THE MOONEYED HOUND

Illustrated by
Jim Marsh

THE MOONEYED HOUND
■
Billy C. Clark

Edited for republication by
James M. Gifford
Patricia A. Hall
Chuck D. Charles

The Jesse Stuart Foundation
Ashland, Kentucky
1995

The Mooneyed Hound

Copyright © 1958 by Billy C. Clark
Copyright © 1986 by Billy C. Clark
Copyright © 1995 by Billy C. Clark

Book Design by FLEXISOFT

All rights reserved. No part of this book may be reproduced or utilized in any form or by any means, electronic or mechanical, including photocopying, or by any information storage or retrieval system, without permission in writing from the publisher.

Library of Congress Cataloging-in-Publication Data

Clark, Billy C. (Billy Curtis)
    Mooneyed hound / by Billy C. Clark ; edited for republication by James M. Gifford, Patricia A. Hall ; illustrated by Jim Marsh.
       p. cm.
    Sequel to: The trail of the hunter's horn.
    Summary: A contest to find the best coon hound in Kentucky tests Jeb's belief in his half-blind dog Mooneye.
    ISBN 0-945084-49-8
    [1. Dogs--Fiction. 2. Contests--Fiction. 3. Kentucky--Fiction.] I. Gifford, James M. II. Hall, Patricia A., 1945- . III. Marsh, Jim, 1933- ill. V. Title.
PZ7.C535Mo   1995   95-7143
                                                          CIP
                                                           AC

Published by:
The Jesse Stuart Foundation
P.O. Box 391
Ashland, KY 41114
1995

To my wife Ruth, my son Billy, my daughter Melissa, my three grandchildren Benjamin, Timothy, and Jodie Elisabeth, and to Earl F. Lockwood, my brother by mutual adoption so many years ago, for whom the Lockwood Series* was named.

*The Lockwood Series includes *The Mooneyed Hound* and it's companion book, *The Trail of the Hunter's Horn.*

CONTENTS

Mooneyed Hound 9

Music of the Horn 24

The Fight 38

The Search for Jeptha 57

The Promise 68

A Trail of Faith 73

A Touch of Faith 79

The Entry 87

The Secret 94

Jeptha Finds a Way 105

The Stubleg Captain 109

The Gift 118

About the Author 137

Chapter One
MOONEYED HOUND
■

Jeb stood in the shade of the large sycamore that shadowed the yard of the small cabin. He looked down the long, crooked trail that wound through the willows on the banks of Catlettscreek. He watched the path for his Uncle Jeptha. Jeptha worked at the timber mill, far up the Big Sandy River. Inside the cabin, Jeb could hear Grandma Quildy humming and, now and then, singing a song.

Beside Jeb stood Lucy, the small redbone hound that belonged to Jeptha. And beside her, lying with his head across his paws, was Mooneye. His coat was as red as the feathers of a redbird and he looked like his mother, Lucy. Mooneye belonged to Jeb.

Now that the pup was nearly full grown, the two hounds looked very much alike, except for the bobtail and mooneye of Jeb's hound. The bobtail was the mark of the pup's father, a bulldog from across the river in West Virginia. And then there was the mooneye. The eye was white as the bark of a sycamore and, according to Jeptha, it was the mark of the moon. Only one dog in a thousand carried the mark of the moon.

A leaf circled through the air and Jeb looked at Mooneye as the pup watched with his good eye. The leaf drifted close to him and fell. Mooneye got up, walked over and sniffed at the leaf. Then he stopped and turned his head toward the path. A low growl came from his throat…Lucy bawled out and started down the path.

"He's here, Grandma Quildy," Jeb hollered. "Uncle Jeptha is here."

Grandma Quildy came out into the yard, wiping her hands with her apron. Jeb had already started down the path, the pup running behind, its long ears flapping like the wings of a hawk.

Farther down the path Jeb could see that Jeptha had squatted to pet Lucy. He could hear Lucy whimper, trying to push her nose into Jeptha's big hands. Her long tail wagged back and fourth in the dust of the path. Mooneye bawled and Jeptha looked up the path. But before Jeptha could speak Jeb said:

"Lucy and Mooneye trailed and killed a wildcat. Mooneye trailed the wildcat all by himself and backed it into a rock cliff and…and…I blowed the horn, Uncle Jeptha. I raised the horn up and

I blowed it. Lucy came over the ridge and..."

"Wait a minute," Jeptha said. "Wait a minute. You're going to blow all the leaves off the trees talking so hard."

Jeptha moved a cloth bandage away from his hound's side and looked at the deep wound. Then he rubbed his hand over the rest of the hound's body, feeling for more wounds. Mooneye was trying to push Lucy out of the way and get closer to Jeptha. Jeptha grinned and patted the pup on the head. The stubtail wagged back and forth.

"Trailed a wildcat, did he?" Jeptha said, shaking his head and rising to his feet. "When we get to the cabin, you will have to tell me all about it."

Mooneye ran up the path sniffing in the dust and poking his nose into the saplings. Lucy walked slower, limping and walking close to Jeptha's feet.

"Take your time, old gal," Jeptha spoke softly to Lucy. "Old Jeptha is here now and he will take care of you."

Jeptha picked Grandma Quildy off the ground and swung her around and around like he always did when he came home.

"Good Lord couldn't have sent you at a better time," Grandma Quildy said, grinning. "That wildcat that Jeb caught keeps getting bigger and bigger all the time and I feared there wouldn't be room left at the cabin." The grin left her face. "It was a dangerous thing, killing that wildcat, and Jeb no bigger than he is, hounds or no hounds."

"Seems to me that I knew a woman once that fought and killed a wildcat with a poker," Jeptha said.

Grandma Quildy's face turned red and she started toward the cabin, shaking her head. She turned at the door and looked back and grinned.

Jeptha squatted again and lifted the cloth bandage on Lucy's side. Jeb was still thinking about the woman who killed the wildcat. Jeb had never heard it mentioned before and he was anxious to hear the story of a woman who would stand toe to toe with a wildcat without a hound nearby.

"Was this wildcat as big as the one the hounds caught, Uncle Jeptha?" Jeb said, hoping that Jeptha would start talking about it and tell him the whole story.

"Well," Jeptha said, looking at Jeb who had squatted beside him, "I didn't see the wildcat the dogs caught the other night, so I can't rightly say. But I remember the other one very well. I was about your size, Jeb. Pa followed the timber back then, same as I do now, and he had gone up the

Big Sandy to raft logs for the fall run. I had heard Pa speak often of the river, calling it the Chatterwaha which meant river of many sandbars according to the Indians. I had begged all day to go back with Pa, and when he left without me I was mad and pouting. I couldn't go to sleep that night, so I lay in the bed listening to the wind in the trees. Then I heard a chicken scream. I jumped out of bed and ran to the window. Ma was heading toward the sycamore with a flashlight and a poker. And down the tree came the biggest wildcat I ever saw. Ma swarped at it and the wildcat dropped the chicken and turned. I saw the teeth of the wildcat and saw the swish of the poker. The wildcat rolled over, turned toward Ma and the poker swished again. The wildcat went down, growling and clawing. I ran from the room without any shoes on and by the time I got to the yard the wildcat was ready for skinning." Jeptha eyed the old sycamore and wiped his face. "One reason I remember it so well was that when Pa came home and found the wildcat, he was determined that we should have a hound. So I got my first hound-dog. And I called him Sermon."

"You mean it was Grandma Quildy?" Jeb said, squinting his eyes toward the cabin. Jeb stared at the door of the cabin and then at the sycamore.

He thought of Grandma Quildy running through the yard. And here at this tree she had stood toe to toe with only a poker against the wildcat. Even a hound might have turned the other way. And then Jeb thought of the many nights he had set by the fire watching Grandma Quildy read from the Bible, stopping now and then to listen to his tale of the wildcat he had killed by the rock cliff. There had always been a smile on her wrinkled face and, as she pushed the long gray-streaked hair away from her face, she would often let her hand slide down to pat the small red pup that was stretched beside her.

"The Lord has been good to you Jeb," she would say. "He has given you a good hunting dog."

She had never mentioned the wildcat she had killed with a poker. Jeb thought of how he had bragged and bragged. There had been times that he knew that the wildcat was not nearly as big as he said it was. But before he had never figured that Grandma Quildy knew much about wildcats, and a big wildcat sounded better to him. Now he felt ashamed of himself.

Jeb turned his eyes from the cabin and watched Jeptha. Grandma Quildy had placed a slice of potato on the wound to draw the infection.

Mooneyed Hound

Now Jeptha removed the potato and tied the bandage firmly in place again.

But Jeb still thought of Grandma Quildy's wildcat. And he thought, too, of the wildcat he had caught at the cliff. He wondered why he had bragged so much. He thought of himself standing back at the rock cliff. He could feel the cool hollow wind against his face and the soft moss under his feet. The long limbs of the beeches brushed against one another and made a low swishing sound. There was the feel of the hunter's horn against his side and the rawhide over his shoulder. And then from the black oak and shellbark hickory on the ridge came the bawl of a hound, drifting down the steep slope. It was the prettiest music Jeb had ever heard.

Maybe these things were the reason he had bragged so loud. He was a hunter and only a hunter could know these things. A hunter had the right to brag and stretch the facts a little. Jeptha had told him this, and Jeptha was the greatest hunter in the world, Jeb thought.

Jeptha stood up and patted Jeb on the shoulder. Then he turned toward the cabin.

"Don't speak a word of what I told you to your Grandma," he said. "She'd be apt to skin me as fast as a hunter would skin a young possum. She cried for days after she killed that wildcat. Her heart is as soft as a mayapple blossom."

As Jeb sat at the supper table he thought again of the wildcat and Grandma Quildy. He set his mind that all of his bragging would be to Jeptha from then on.

After Jeb had finished eating he went with Jeptha up the creek to gather pokeberry roots. Jeptha said that he could make a medicine from these roots to heal the wound on Lucy's side. Jeb walked close to Jeptha, and as he walked he looked at the deep prints Jeptha made in the soft mud of the creekbank. Jeb looked back at his own tracks and they looked as light as the tracks of a sparrow. One day, Jeb thought, his tracks would go deep in the mud like Jeptha's.

Mooneye ran in the lead, poking his nose in and out of the willows. His stubtail twisted back and forth and his long ears flapped up and down. All of a sudden Mooneye whined and began to work faster. Jeptha held out his hand and stopped. Jeb stood beside him and watched the red pup. Lucy started toward Mooneye but Jeptha told her to stay. She lowered her head and eyed the pup. She wagged her long tail and looked up at Jeptha with sad eyes. She whined and looked at Jeptha as if she were begging to go see what had made the trail. But she would not move against Jeptha's word.

"The pup has scented a muskrat," Jeptha said. "Let's see how he works a trail."

Mooneye moved slowly, the stubtail now wagging back and forth so fast that it was hard to see. Now and then he stopped and threw his head in the air and whined. He did not open like he had when he had trailed the wildcat. He stuck his nose to the ground again and moved through the willow grove into an open cornfield. Moving away from the edge of the field, he worked his way between two large shocks of corn. At the far shock he stopped and stuck his nose into the air. He lifted his head high and his bugle voice drifted across the bottom.

"My word," Jeptha said. "The voice of Lucy."

Jeb's chest swelled with pride and his heart beat fast. Out of the other end of the shock came the muskrat. It was not often that a muskrat came out to search for food during the day, and so at first Jeb had figured it was a cold trail. Now he realized that the trail being so hot should have been reason enough for Mooneye to know that something was at the end of it. The fat muskrat wobbled across the field toward the creek. Mooneye spotted it and he bawled again and started chasing it by sight instead of scent. Jeb knew that this was the mark of a young hound. A true hound followed only by scent and for a minute Jeb felt ashamed of the pup. Lucy had spotted the rat and she started to break but Jeptha spoke again. She held. Jeptha was grinning and chuckling out loud. The muskrat cut through the willows and circled the end of a log that had been pushed up on the bank by high water. At the end of the log he turned and slid into the water of the creek. Jeb watched the muskrat glide beneath the surface. Mooneye was close behind, lifting his head to bawl to Jeb. The red pup lowered his nose and sniffed the hot scent. He made the quick turn at the end of the log. But the log faced the blind eye of the pup and as he swung his head he crashed into it. He yelped and lost his footing on the bank and tumbled into the creek. Up he came, his paws striking the water and he swam back to shore. Jeb stooped on the bank and lifted up the pup. A small stream of blood dripped from the side of Mooneye's face.

"He couldn't see the log," Jeb said, a quiver in his voice.

Jeptha stooped down beside the pup and looked at the small cut.

"You better learn to trail by scent, little fellow,"

he said. "Run by sight and we'll be putting poke root juice on you instead of Lucy."

Jeptha patted the pup on the head and started up the creek. He did not stop again until he came to a grove of sugar maples. Poke grew beneath the shade of the maple tree. The small sapling willows and the weedy limbs were covered with small red pokeberries. Jeptha took out his knife and dug after the roots. After he had gathered enough, he turned toward the cabin.

At the cabin Jeptha boiled the roots in water and then strained the juice into a small jar. Jeb watched him dip a white cloth into the jar and then dab the juice on Lucy's wound. Lucy whimpered as if she were in pain, but she stood trembling beside Jeptha. She would not move because Jeptha had told her to stay. As Jeb watched he thought again of the blind eye of his pup.

"Do you reckon," Jeb said after a while, "if you was to put some of the poke herb on the white eye of my hound that it would cause him to see out of it?"

Jeptha looked at Jeb and frowned. "That dog is one in a thousand. Now do you reckon I would take its mooneye away with a dab of poke juice?"

For a minute Jeb felt ashamed that he had

asked. He had not wanted to take the mark away. What he wanted was for the pup to see. The pup had run into the log back at the creek because he was blind in one eye, and Jeb knew he would be apt to do it again and again.

Still, Jeb had not forgotten what Jeptha said about Lucy's pup. According to Jeptha, Lucy had chased and caught the moon from the tallest ridge of the mountain. In return, the moon had marked her pup with the sign of the night. Jeb was not ungrateful. It was just that he felt sorry for Mooneye.

"Maybe not take out the chip of the moon?" Jeb said. "Maybe you could put just enough to take away the darkness from before it."

"Does a hound-dog trail with its eye, Jeb?" Jeptha asked.

"Nope," Jeb said.

"Far as I know," Jeptha said, "there is not another dog in Kentucky that carries the mark of the moon. And to my way of thinking, there ain't another hound in the hills besides Lucy that would take up the trail of a wildcat and manage to hold it alone. The pup has the markings of a true hound, Jeb. A hound never lived that carried the bugle voice of Lucy until she fetched this pup. With age he will become more sure on the trail and will not overrun it. Today he was running by sight and he hit the log because he was moving too fast and paying no attention to the trail. Maybe it was a good thing. He will learn to be more careful."

After Jeptha had placed the cloth back over the wound, Lucy wagged her long tail and licked Jeptha's hand. She moved slowly across the yard. Her side was still very sore.

"I will take Lucy back to the timber mill with me this time," Jeptha said, watching her walk to the end of the yard and curl in the grass. "Now that the logs are almost rafted, I will have time to care for her. Besides, she would be of no use to you here, with her not being able to follow the trail."

At daybreak the next day Jeptha packed his things and stood at the door of the cabin. "Will you be gone long this time?" Grandma Quildy asked her son.

"Only a short while," Jeptha said. "We are working close by. The logs are tied at Buchanan, about ten mile from here. The river will swell over the banks toward the last of the month and we will ride the logs to the mouth of the Sandy. Then I'll be back."

"I'll pray for you, Jeptha," Grandma Quildy said, reaching high to pat his big shoulders with her wrinkled hand.

"Now don't go to worrying, Ma," Jeptha said. "Jeb, here, is a man now. Caught his first wildcat. He can take care of things while I'm gone."

"Ain't worrying none," Grandma Quildy said. "Your Pa was a timber man, always coming and going like the leaves on the trees, restless as the wind. Riding logs down the river is dangerous."

"I'll be careful," Jeptha said.

"And my praying will guide you," Grandma Quildy said, turning into the other room.

Lucy stood eyeing Jeptha and Jeptha looked down at her and smiled.

"You will go this trip, Lucy," Jeptha said, and he started down the path.

Lucy started down the path in a run and then, slowed by the soreness again, she dropped back and walked beside Jeptha.

"About the horn, Jeb," Jeptha said, stopping at the edge of the willow grove, "it is your job to train the pup to it. Remember that a hound must turn only to its sound. And it is not an easy job to break a hound from a trail when the scent is hot. No two horns will ever sound the same. Once a hound learns the sound of his master's horn, he will remember it and will turn to its sound and no other."

Jeb walked with Jeptha to the willow grove.

"About the mooneye, Jeb," he said. "There is a reason for it. Whatever the pup has lost in the blind eye he will gain it back in some other place. And that is in the print of your Grandma Quildy's Bible."

Jeb watched Jeptha go out of sight, and then he returned to the cabin. It seemed strange, he thought, that Jeptha would know what was in the print of Grandma Quildy's Book. He had never spoken of it before. Strange, too, what he said about the pup's mooneye.

At the cabin, Jeb looked at Grandma Quildy as she sat beside the fire grate. She was reading from the Bible and Jeb knew that she was asking the Lord to guide Jeptha along the tramroads to the timber mill. Why would a big man like Jeptha need help from such a small book, he wondered.

Chapter Two
MUSIC OF THE HORN
■

Jeb stood on the slope and looked across the cornfield. He wiped his face. Then he folded the ragweed cord he had been using to tie the corn in shock and stuck it in his pocket. There was a difference in the wind now, and Jeb was glad that the field work was done. It was not the warm summer wind that waved young sprouts of corn back and forth. This wind shook the leaves from the trees and rustled the blades of corn in the shock. This, Jeb knew, was the wind of frost, and also the wind of the hunter. It would change the fur of the coon and possum to a winter coat and would bring snow to the hills. The snow would hold the trails of all the animals so that Jeb could follow.

The sun was slowly breaking over the ridge and the frost still covered the highest blade of grass. Jeb looked across the field to where the red pup was sniffing along the corn stubble. Morning glories grew to the top of the stubble, the vines were as thick as the vines of the wild honeysuckle.

And from each vine hung the blue flowers that Jeb loved to see. The morning glory was one of the few flowers of the hills that could stand against the frost and open each morning without the sun's touch.

Jeb waited until Mooneye was at the far end of the field and then he called. The red pup raised his head and turned toward Jeb. With his ears flopping in the air he came running. When he reached Jeb, Jeb scolded him and the red hound hunkered and whined.

"You have got to learn to quit coming to the sound of my voice," Jeb scolded.

Jeb motioned the pup across the field again. Mooneye crossed the field and worked the ground with his nose. After a short while, Jeb raised the horn to his lips and blew. The music of the horn drifted over the slope. The pup jerked his head and a smile came to Jeb's face. The hound had turned and he crossed the field as fast as he could run and stopped at Jeb's feet. Jeb stooped, patted his head and bragged on his good dog. The pup sniffed the horn and jumped up and down.

"Reckon you sure enough like the horn, don't you, Mooneye?" Jeb said proudly. "Reckon you know that no one but a hunter can blow it. Jeptha said this. And I reckon he knows more about hunting than anyone else in the valley."

The red hound whimpered and wagged his stubtail.

"I reckon me and you are sure enough hunters now," Jeb said, patting the pup on the head again.

The pup turned and Jeb looked again at his white eye. For a minute he frowned. Once again the white eye did not seem to be the mark of the moon; it was a mark of blindness. Jeb did not like to think of the blind eye, so he motioned the pup across the field again.

The pup was learning fast. At night, Jeb worked him along the bottoms and low on the slopes where the possum traveled. Mooneye was quick to find their track and open-voiced on the trail. His voice was as deep as Lucy's. Every time he listened, Jeb's chest swelled and he loved the little red hound more. Mooneye had learned many of the habits of the possum. Already he knew that the possum trail would almost always lead to a tree. And so when the pup could no longer find the scent on the ground, he began to search the bark of the closest tree where the track had ended. When he caught the scent on the bark of the tree he would stand and bawl until Jeb came.

The first night he had treed, he had chewed the bark on a young beech sapling that held the

Music of the Horn

possum until the white flesh of the inner wood looked as white under the beam of Jeb's flashlight as a creek-washed gravel. Jeb waited until Mooneye started chewing again and then he scolded him and smacked him across the nose. Too many good hounds had worn their teeth to the gum by chewing bark. When a hound was chewing bark, he could not watch the tree and the game could easily slip out on him. Also, a hound would need sharp teeth if he were to fight a coon. A coon would not play dead like a possum. Mooneye had chewed only two trees before he learned it was wrong.

One night Mooneye struck the trail of a possum below the cabin and he bawled to tell Jeb. Jeb listened to the sound. He knew the pup was working slow on the trail. The baying became deeper and each time further away. Jeb could tell that the pup was following a hot track. In a short while, from high on the slope, came the bugle voice of the treed hound. Jeb lifted the horn to his lips and looked into the dark timbers. Now was the time, he thought, to try the sound of the horn with the pup close to game. Jeb raised the horn and blew with all his might, and then he lowered the horn and waited. He listened as the music of the horn drifted from the valley, climbed the steep slope to the high ridge, and echoed back from the next valley. The barking stopped. Jeb smiled and shook his head. Mooneye was coming in, he thought. Then, back on the slope came the bugle voice of the hound. Jeb listened close. Each bark came from the same place; from the tree where Mooneye had driven the possum. Jeb swung the horn across his shoulder and started toward the tree.

At the tree, the red pup sat on his haunches. His head was in the air. When he saw Jeb he bawled louder and louder and began to run around the tree. Now and then he leaped upon the tree trying to sink his claws into the bark and climb, but each time he slipped and fell to the ground.

"Mooneye!" Jeb hollered. "You didn't come to the sound of the horn like you was supposed to do!"

Mooneye turned his head sideways and looked at Jeb. And then he bawled and leaped again upon the tree.

Jeb walked a short piece from the tree and raised the horn. He blew a short blast. But still the pup circled the tree.

"Mooneye!" Jeb shouted.

The red hound turned and walked toward Jeb. Jeb patted him on the head and the pup ran back

Music of the Horn

to the tree. Jeb called the pup twice more and then he turned and walked down the slope. Standing where he had first heard the hound, Jeb lifted the horn and blew with all his might. Then he waited. The sound of the horn died in the woods and there was no sound now except the wind in the trees. Jeb worried and started to walk back to the tree. Just then he heard Mooneye in the underbrush. He came to Jeb, whined, and wagged his stubtail. Then he looked toward the woods. Jeb stooped, hugged Mooneye's neck and spoke soft words. Then he looked up the slope.

"Okay, Mooneye," Jeb said. "Go get him."

The red hound threw his head into the air and disappeared. In a short while, Jeb again heard the bugle voice. It sounded further away than the first tree had been. But Mooneye was treed.

The possum had sneaked from the beech while the hound had traveled to the sound of the horn. But Mooneye had found his track again and had pushed him up a small oak. Jeb shined the light on the possum. Next, he placed the light on the ground and put a rock under the end to raise the beam to the possum and then Jeb shinnied up the tree.

The possum hung to a small limb at the top. As Jeb shook the limb, it looked at him and made

Music of the Horn

a low growling sound. Jeb shook as hard as he could. The long tail of the possum was wrapped around the limb and the possum held fast. On the ground Mooneye jumped up and down and bawled into the air. Jeb shook and shook and down came the possum. Jeb slid down the tree.

The possum lay on the ground, and around the possum circled the red hound. He was not moving in like Jeb had thought he would, but he was staying at a distance growling and showing his teeth. His head was turned to one side as if he were favoring his blind eye, the same as he had done the night he had pushed the wildcat to the cliff. Jeb stooped beside the pup and patted him on the head.

"Get him," Jeb said.

The red hound caught the possum in one leap. Jeb's eyes were wide. He had never seen the pup so vicious. He snarled and growled and moved back and forth as fast as the wind. Jeb heard the snap of the sharp teeth. Mooneye's red hair bristled and in his good eye Jeb could see the redness of fire. Mooneye is a true hound, Jeb thought, a coon hound.

Jeb put the possum in a sack and started for the cabin. Mooneye followed at his side and when he turned to work the woods again Jeb scolded him. The pup would have to learn when the hunt was over, Jeb thought. Only poor hunters had to chase their hounds when they were ready to go home. Mooneye walked beside Jeb all the way back to the cabin.

Grandma Quildy was sitting beside the fire as Jeb walked in. She looked up.

"The woods were full of the sounds of the hound and the horn," she said. "Did you fetch any game?"

"I caught a possum," Jeb said, holding the sack out.

"My word," Grandma Quildy said, grinning and placing a pine split between the pages of the Book she was reading. "Just when I was getting a taste for possum and sweet potatoes. I will dress him tonight. There is sure enough a hunter around the cabin."

Jeb handed her the sack and walked behind her to the kitchen. In what seemed like just a few seconds, Grandma Quildy had jerked the hide from the possum. She held the skinned possum over a pan and shook her head.

"My, but he's a fat one," she said. "That Mooneye has got eyes for the fat ones, I'll bet."

Jeb thought about this. The pup had only one good eye. The other eye was white as the bark of the sycamore. In it was nothing but darkness. The hound seemed to have the makings of a fine coon dog, except for the white eye. To Jeb, his bugle voice seemed louder than Lucy's. He was faster than Lucy and much more powerful. The red coat, keen nose, and bugle voice were from Lucy. But here it stopped. His chest was already broader than Lucy's and bore the signs of the bulldog. His jaws hung over the lower lip. This could be either the marking of a hound or a bulldog. The broad head did not look like a hound, that is, except for the long ears. And there was the stubtail. Jeb remembered once that Jeptha had laughed and said: "Whoever heard of a bobtailed hound?" Tears had welled in Jeb's eyes when he saw that the small pup had no tail. But Jeptha had told him that the tail was like a short-butted oak; the fewer the limbs, the stronger the trunk. And Jeptha had been right. Jeb did not think that there was another dog in the hills as strong as his red hound.

"Grandma Quildy," Jeb said. "Does a hound-dog have faith?"

Grandma Quildy laid the skinned possum in a pan and turned to face Jeb.

"Why, Jeb?" she asked.

"I thought that maybe somewhere in the print

of the Bible you had read where they might have," Jeb said.

Grandma Quildy frowned, squinted her eyes and looked toward the window.

"I don't believe I recollect words in the Bible that say that," she said. "What is the reason, Jeb?"

Jeb did not look at Grandma Quildy. Once Grandma Quildy, he remembered, had spoke of the blind man Samson. Samson was the strongest man in the world and had the most faith. But then, he had lost his faith and no longer believed in the word of the Bible. He became blind and was left to wander among the tall trees of the mountains. Blind Samson had followed the sound of Gabriel's horn as Mooneye might follow the sound of Jeb's. For his faith, the Lord had given Samson back his sight.

"I thought maybe," Jeb said, "maybe that if Mooneye was to have enough faith that the Lord might do him like he did Samson. Maybe he would take away the darkness and put light in my dog's blind eye."

Grandma Quildy looked at Jeb. She pulled her apron to her face and wiped her eyes.

"God bless you, Jeb," she said, "I don't rightly know if it is in the Book or not, but as soon as I clean this possum I'll look and see." Grandma

Quildy stared at the possum and then rubbed her hand over her chin. "Maybe, Jeb...maybe It would say that it was the place of the dog's master to have enough faith for it. If this be true, a man would have to have twice as much faith. I'll look carefully. But there is one thing I know without looking again; what the Lord takes from us He takes for a purpose. It ain't right to question why. It ought to be about the same with a hound-dog; the Lord made them too. So it is to my figuring that He took the eye and He had His reason."

"But why would He want to take the eye of my pup?" Jeb said.

Grandma Quildy wiped her hands with her apron and looked again toward Jeb.

"The Bible speaks of a man, Jeb," she said, "by the name of Job. And, Job, it tells, was a rich man. He owned more land than your eyes could see from the top of a mountain. Cattle and sheep grazed on his land as thick as blackberries. Now Job loved the Lord with all his might, and he had a lot of faith. But one day the Lord wanted to see how much faith Job had, so He sent a great storm to the mountains. The wind and rain tore down the tall trees and killed all the cattle and sheep. At first, Job did not lose his faith, and he turned his eyes toward the dark clouds and said: 'Blessed

The Mooneyed Hound

be the name of the Lord.'" Grandma Quildy wiped her forehead and pushed her hair away from her face. "But then Job began to lose his faith. People began to mock the loss of Job's land, just as there have been some that have mocked the mooneye of your hound. Why, they asked Job, if he had been such a good man had the Lord taken from him? And Job began to wonder. Finally he questioned the Lord. 'Job,' the Lord said, 'does the horse pull out the black oak stumps from the clay hillside because of the strength you have given him? Or, does the hawk circle the mountain top because you tell it to fly?' And Job knew that the horse was given strength by the Lord, and the hawk circled the mountain top because the Lord wanted it to. Job knew that the Lord had great powers and that He had taken from Job for a reason and Job felt ashamed. And don't you know, Jeb, right then and there the Lord gave Job back more land than you could see from the top of two mountains. Cattle and sheep, thicker then the berries of the elderberry brush that shades the waters of the creek, grazed his land."

"But why did the Lord take the things from Job in the first place if Job had faith and loved him, Grandma Quildy?" Jeb asked, squinting his eyes and looking at her.

Music of the Horn

"There is a reason why the Lord takes, Jeb," Grandma Quildy said. "We are told the story of Job so that we might know He does and then we won't have to question like Job. Maybe there is reason for the eye of the pup. It could be He marked the hound with the eye of the moon so that other little mooneyed pups that He lifts out of the clouds and sets on the mountain ridge won't have to wonder why their eye is as white as the bark of the sycamore. Maybe through your pup they will be told, just as we are told from the story of Job. But I will look closer for you for sure. Just remember, Jeb, what the Lord takes away from the white eye of the hound, he will give back twofold if you have enough faith."

"But how will I know if Mooneye has faith if it is not in the print of the Book?" Jeb said.

"I reckon," Grandma Quildy said, "if you was wanting to be sure then you would have to strengthen your faith until it is double. And then, Jeb, perhaps you would have the faith of Job."

Chapter Three
THE FIGHT
∎

It was not long before Jeb began to think that whatever had been taken from the pup's eye had been put into his nose. Mooneye became slower on the trail and not a possum in the hills was able to fool him. He traveled over stumps, walked logs, and waded streams to push his game to a tree. At the tree he would freeze and wait until Jeb came or blew the horn. Jeb could shout at the top of his voice but only the bawl of the hound would answer him. In fact, he would stand within seeing distance of the tree and try to call the red hound away from the game, but the dog paid no attention. Yet with one blast of the hunter's horn the hound would turn and come to his young master.

Or perhaps if the great nose was not an exchange for the eye, it could have been his voice. Mooneye was not a big dog. He was long and lean, except for his broad chest. The long ears on the short, stubby head looked almost out of place on the red hound. And the stubtail and mooneye

The Fight

marked him from all other dogs of the mountain. It was hard to believe that the deep bugle voice could have come from so small a dog. The deepest hollow could not pin it in, and it rolled up the slope and along the high ridge like thunder squeezed through a hollow log. And Jeb was not the only one to hear and brag about the bugle voice. Mr. Tate, owner of the store where Grandma Quildy traded, said that Mooneye's bugle voice was the prettiest he had ever heard.

"Deep as the voice of Lucy," he told Jeb. "And apt to get deeper than hers one day, if it ain't already."

And more than once hunters that Jeb met in the hills had stopped to brag on the bobtailed hound. That is, all hunters except Bunt Borders. Bunt was a fox hunter and Jeb figured that he was only jealous because his foxhounds did not have the bugle voice of the red hound. Jeb met him often at Mr. Tate's store and Bunt always had something to say about the mooneye and stubtail. Jeb had learned to pay little attention, although he had asked Grandma Quildy about Bunt's teasing.

"Men laughed at Samson," she told Jeb. "They mocked his blindness too, and the Lord gave him the eyes of an eagle."

Jeb said no more about the eye, but often he wondered if one day the Lord might give the red hound the eyes of an eagle. One thing he was now sure of. He must never question what the good Lord might be intending.

Jeb had trained Mooneye on possum and skunk, waiting until he became wiser on the trail before he gave him freedom to trail the coon. The coon was clever and different from the skunk and possum in many ways. A coon would run half the night sometimes before he took to a tree. A possum would run only a short while, usually to the nearest tree if the hound was close. And the coon moved fast, stopping only long enough to fool a hound. Sometimes the coon would leap to the side of a tree, strike the bark to leave his scent, and then push himself off the side of the tree and land perhaps ten feet away. And when the hound came to the end of the trail he would strike the scent on the tree. And here the hound would stop and bark treed and his master would spend half the night trying to shine the light on a coon that was not in the tree but probably two hollows away listening to the bawl of the hound he had fooled. Only a smart hound, seasoned to the trail and trained by a smart master, would circle the tree to see if the coon had slipped out before he barked

The Fight

treed. Another trick of the coon was to wade in water, or swim and come out on the far banks. There was no scent left on the surface of water and many a hound would lose the trail and stop. Only a good hound would know what to do. The smart hound would search the other side of the stream and find where the coon had come out of the water. And here the chase would start again.

A coon did not sulk like a possum. The coon was vicious and once trapped by a hound he would turn to fight. The powerful feet with claws a half inch long could rake through the hide of a hound like a knife, and his powerful teeth could tear out a handful of flesh in one bite.

The last trick of the coon was the most dangerous of all, and the most feared by the hunter, especially if the hound was young. This trick was to wait in the middle of a stream to fight, which meant almost certain death to a hound. In water, it took a smart dog to kill a coon. A coon was almost as much at home in the water as he was under the trees. And in the water the coon would sink his teeth into the dog and pull him under to drown.

The scent of coons was not new to Mooneye. Often he had struck their trail and Jeb had let him run, but always Jeb had lifted the horn to his lips and called him off the trail. The hound came in whimpering and waiting for Jeb to motion him on, but Jeb had waited.

As Jeb stood in the yard of the cabin looking up toward the steep slope he was thinking of the coon. The only green on the hills now was in the green needles of the pine tree. The winter wind had shaken the leaves from the other trees and they cracked under Jeb's feet. Dusk was moving down the slope and already it was too dark to see to the top of the ridge. The clouds were dark and hovered over the mountain top like the black wings of a crow. Earlier there had been a light rain and this was a sign that tonight would be a good night to hunt in the woods. It would be a perfect night for coon to travel. All day Jeb thought about going hunting, because tonight would be more than just another night in the woods. Jeb set his mind that if Mooneye struck the track of a coon tonight he would let him trail it. If Mooneye should tree the coon, then Jeb would climb the tree and shake it out and let the pup go in to fight. Jeb knew that it was no longer right to let the hound run for hours and then call him off when he was close to his game. The red hound was old enough to be on his own.

If he had to, Jeb thought, he could help the

The Fight

pup fight the coon. He could use a stick and be like Grandma Quildy was with the poker. Jeb looked toward the sycamore. The long bare limbs stretched over the yard. And then he looked again toward the hills. By the time he got down the creek and into the hollow to hunt, it would be dark enough under the beech trees to use a flashlight. Jeb walked into the cabin and lifted the hunter's horn from the mantle over the fire grate. Grandma Quildy looked up from the Bible.

"Hunt low on the slopes, Jeb," she said. "There's a keenness to the wind. There are signs of a storm. You ought to stay close enough to get to the shelter of the cabin. The woods is no place for a hunter during a storm. Already there is a heavy wind in the trees."

Jeb walked out into the yard. Mooneye saw the hunter's horn and he lifted his head into the air and bawled. He twisted his head toward the willow grove and started down the path, sniffing the ground.

Jeb stepped out of the willow grove into the mouth of a small hollow and stopped under a grove of beech trees that grew low on the slope. He checked his flashlight again and shined it into one of the trees. A bird, roosting under a pod of brown leaves, fluttered out of the tree. Jeb listened to it strike limbs as it flew through the thick beech limbs, blind in the dark. Mooneye cocked his head to one side, listened, and then looked up at Jeb and whimpered to go.

"Go get him, Mooneye," Jeb said, pointing at the small creek where Jeb figured a coon was apt to be searching for crawdads. Mooneye threw his head sideways and disappeared from sight.

Jeb stood alone under the trees. A tree frog bellowed from along the creek and another bird fluttered from a limb somewhere. The night was dark and quiet and Jeb sat down on a log and waited for Mooneye to circle.

A half hour later Jeb rose from the log and stretched. Mooneye had been gone a long time without coming in. The hollow wind was getting colder and Jeb moved close to a large beech, so that he could shelter from the wind that moved down the small creek. A light spray of rain struck the beech limbs and Jeb uneasily got back to his feet. Mooneye had been gone too long. It was not likely that he would try to work to the end of the creek in one circle. Jeb leaned against the side of the beech and looked through the darkness, up the creek. The sound of the water bubbling over the sand rock of the hill was all he heard. Jeb dropped his hand to his side and touched the

The Fight

hunter's horn. If Mooneye had not struck a trail on the creek by this time, he thought, he was not apt to do it now. Perhaps the coon had gone to the ridge tonight to work in ground where a cornfield had stood during the summer. Jeb looked toward the dark clouds. There wasn't a lot of time left for him to hunt. Grandma Quildy would be worried about him. He could climb up the slope, circle the ridge, and work back toward the cabin. If he should strike a trail close to the cabin, Grandma Quildy could hear the hound and would know that Jeb was close and she would probably not mind his staying out and listening to the hound. Jeb did not like to call Mooneye in, but he knew that he should be working toward the ridge. And so he lifted the horn.

As he started to blow the horn, Jeb heard the bugle voice of Mooneye. He lowered the horn and listened. Down the creek it came, drifting like a strong wind, taking both sides of the slope. And then the bawl came again. It was long and keen and Jeb knew that Mooneye had struck a trail. Judging from the sound, Jeb figured Mooneye to be almost at the end of the branch. He was trailing, and trailing slow, working a scent. The bawls came one after another and each time further away. Jeb knew it was not a possum.

A possum would have treed before now. And Mooneye was having trouble with the track, but his bark told Jeb that the scent was hot. Jeb looked through the trees and waited.

The red hound turned out of the branch and trailed up the slope toward the ridge. And then the baying stopped. Jeb waited for Mooneye to pick up the track. After a while Jeb became uneasy, and he touched the horn again. But down the slope rolled the voice of the hound. This time the bawls were long and fast and Jeb thought that Mooneye could see the game he was running. Up the slope they went. Jeb listened for the long bawl of the tree. And finally it came. Jeb listened close to make sure that the hound was not still running. Mooneye was sure now and he bawled as he had never bawled before.

Jeb swallowed hard and started up the slope toward the tree. Now it would be his job. The pup had trailed his game like a true hound and had pushed the coon to a tree. Now he would wait for Jeb to come and shake it out on the ground where the hound would have an equal chance. As Jeb cut through the beech grove and under the short oak that poked out of the red clay of the ridge, he became afraid. He did not fear climbing the tree to shake out the coon.

The Fight

He could climb any tree in the hills. He had climbed the shellbark hickory to shake out the nuts after the first frost had seasoned them, and the shellbark hickory was the hardest of all trees to climb. But once on the ground the coon would be left to the hound, at least until Jeb could climb from the tree. Once on the ground the coon would turn to fight. If it was an old coon, there was a good chance that it had fought before, and because it was still alive was proof that it had won. The pup, young and unwise to the tricks of a coon, was apt to rush the coon too fast. And this would be what an old coon would want. Rolling over on his back, he would wait for the hound to straddle him and then, with his powerful claws, he would rip the hound's stomach open and travel safe to his den while the dog lay dying.

Maybe it was too soon to let the pup try the coon, Jeb thought. He could let the hound bark a while at the tree and then call him off. But then, Jeb remembered the night the pup had moved in on the possum. He had not charged it fast; even on the almost helpless possum the hound had moved with caution. He had sized up the possum with his good eye and waited for a chance to grab its throat. There had been enough viciousness in the hound to mark him a fighting hound. Maybe

The Mooneyed Hound

it was the blind eye, Jeb thought, that had held him back to judge his game before he struck, and gave him the caution that it took to be a great hound. The red hound deserved the right to fight the game he had tracked over logs and through thick underbrush to the tree. And Jeb knew it.

Jeb was on the ridge now and he turned out the path that would lead him to the hound's voice. But as Jeb turned, the bawl of the hound stopped. Jeb stood on the ridge and waited. It was not like the hound to leave a tree. Maybe he was circling the tree to be sure, Jeb thought, and he will open up again with his bugle voice. Jeb breathed hard from the climb up the slope and he waited.

The bark came again. But not from the tree. The hound was running down the slope and the track was hot. Jeb swallowed hard. It was sure enough a coon—and an old one. The coon had marked the tree and slipped out to fool the hound. But he had not fooled the hound long. Mooneye had made a circle and had picked it up again where the coon had leaped and was following the coon toward the branch. Jeb listened to the hound. Down the slope he went, into the branch, and up the other side of the hill. And then once again Jeb heard the bawl of the treed hound. But before he could start toward it, Mooneye trailed again. Once

The Fight

again he headed toward the branch. And in the branch this time he turned toward the mouth of the hollow, toward where Jeb had first entered the woods. He was following the small stream toward Catlettscreek.

There was no doubt now; it was an old coon. He had not been able to lose the hound on the hill and he was leading him to water. Mooneye was fast on the trail and the coon knew it. On the ground, the coon must have known that he would be no equal to the speed of the trailing hound. The great nose of the bobtailed pup was fast to catch the scent. But the coon, being old and wise to the noise of a hound, had laid his plan. By barking the tree he had slowed the pup, allowing him more time to reach the large stream of water ahead of him.

The hound was moving fast. Jeb listened to the change of his bark. It was not the long bawl of a slow trail now. The bawls were short and sharp and sounded almost like a scream. On the end of some of the barks, Jeb could hear the vicious growl that came from the hound's throat. If the pup was as close as Jeb thought he was, the coon would make it to the stream and no farther. Should the pup go into the water, there was little chance that he would ever come out. The coon, knowing now

The Mooneyed Hound

that he had misjudged the great nose of the young hound that trailed him, would coax the dog into the stream and fight. Here the coon was apt to win.

Jeb ran as fast as he could to the end of the ridge and stood on the bluff, overlooking the mouth of the hollow. He raised the horn to his lips and blew with all his might. The music of the horn carried over the valley and echoed against the hills. Jeb was close enough to the cabin for Grandma Quildy to hear the horn. But the pup did not turn. The sound of the horn settled in the trees and only the bawl of the hound broke the silence of the hills. Jeb blew again and this time he ran down the slope toward the creek. The only chance to save the red hound, Jeb thought, was to call him from the trail before he reached the water. Jeb stopped in the hollow to catch his breath. He pushed the horn into his belt so that it would not flap against his side when he ran or catch in the low tree limbs. The pup had not turned to the sound of the horn and Jeb was mad. But when he thought of the pup going over the bank and into the water—the coon waiting in the middle of the stream—his anger disappeared. All Jeb could think of was saving the mooneyed hound.

The Fight

Through the trees came one long bawl of the hound. On the end of the bawl was a scream and then it ended. Jeb looked around him. The woods were dark and quiet. He waited again for Mooneye to break the silence with his bugle voice. But he heard only the slow-moving sound of the water from the creek. A light wind rushed through the tree limbs and, up the creek, a tree frog bellowed.

"Mooneye!" Jeb hollered, and he ran toward the willow grove.

There was no sound now to lead Jeb to the trail and he ran wildly through the willow grove toward the creek. Out of breath again, he stopped and wiped tears from his eyes. He shined the light through the thick willow grove and brought the beam back along the soft mud on the banks of the creek. Jeb stood so close to the creek he could hear the water of a smaller stream empty into it. Jeb squinted his eyes along the beam of light. He jerked his head and held the light still. In the soft mud of the branch he saw a track.

Jeb walked over and bent to his knees. It was the track of the hound. Jeb looked at another track beside it. This track looked like the small foot of a barefoot human. Jeb looked again and he swallowed hard. He wiped tears from his eyes as they streamed down his face. This was the largest

The Mooneyed Hound

coon track Jeb had ever seen. Jeb jumped to his feet and followed the small stream. He didn't stop until he stood on the banks of Catlettscreek. And here he flashed the light along the mud bank.

Close to a water soaked log he found tracks. The track of the coon led into the water. Jeb frowned and with his arm wiped his eyes again. Beside the track of the coon, pushed into the soft mud and leading into the water, were the tracks of the mooneyed hound.

Jeb sat down on the bank and cried. The wind shook the limbs of the low-hanging willows, and pushed the water of the stream against the mud banks. There was no sound or sight of the coon or the hound. The coon, Jeb thought, was now safe in his den. The red hound, Jeb thought, was on the bottom of the stream, brushing along the sand bottom, drifting with the current like a watersoaked log. Jeb wiped his eyes and he let his hand fall to his side. It touched the hunter's horn. Jeb ran his hand along the curve of the horn and up the rawhide strap. There was a chance, he thought, that the hound had crossed the stream and had turned to a silent trail. Tears came to Jeb's eyes. Mooneye, he knew, was an open trailer, and with the scent of the coon on the tip of his nose he would bugle his music over the mountains.

The Fight

There might be some chance, Jeb hoped.

Jeb remembered the story of Job that Grandma Quildy had told him from the print of the Bible. The Lord had taken from Job more land than could be seen from the top of a mountain. He had taken sheep and cattle that were worth a heap of money. From Jeb, it could be that He had taken only a mooneyed, stubtailed hound. And when Jeb thought of the red hound, he wanted to scream through the willows and ask why the small hound that he loved had been taken. But he remembered again that Job had questioned the Lord. Jeb could see the strong horse strain its shoulders and lift the mighty roots of the black oak out of the red clay of the mountain. He thought of the hawk that could circle all day around the top of a mountain without swooping to rest on a tree limb. The Lord, not Job, had given them this power. Job must have been sad, Jeb thought, when he had lost his land and cattle. Perhaps, like Jeb, he had even sat down and cried. One thing Jeb knew for sure: Job had not lost his faith. Instead, he had turned his eyes toward the heavens and said: "Blessed be the name of the Lord."

For this faith the Lord had given Job more land than could be seen from the top of two mountains and had put cattle and sheep there,

The Fight

thicker than the berries of the elderberry bush. All Jeb wanted was the small red hound.

The Lord was surely a great Man, Jeb thought. And he turned his head toward the ridge. Tears welled in his eyes. To Job, he thought, saying "blessed be the name of the Lord" must have been the hardest words he had ever spoken. But it was the best way for Job to show his faith. To Jeb perhaps the hardest thing was to blow the horn and not get an answer from the red hound. But it would be the greatest way Jeb knew to show his faith. So he raised the horn to his lips and blew with all his might. Jeb got to his feet and turned to go out of the willows. He stopped. He heard something. He listened to be sure that it was no the sound of the wind or the water. Jeb's heart beat fast and tears again came to his eyes. The sound was the whine of a dog. Jeb pushed through the willows toward the sound. A short way up the creek, Jeb stopped.

At the edge of the bank, under a clump of willows, stood the red pup. He was trembling and his face was covered with blood. Beside him lay the coon--dead. Jeb could see where the hound had dragged the coon from the water, up through the brush to dry land. Mooneye had fought the coon in water, and he had killed it. Then he had pulled the coon to dry land to keep until Jeb came. The hound stood soaking wet, his red hair parted down his back. Jeb shined the light on the head of the pup. Jeb knew now why the pup had not come to the sound. Blood covered both eyes, and from his good eye hung a sliver of skin where the coon had set his teeth.

The pup was blind.

"Mooneye!" Jeb hollered, and ran toward the pup.

Mooneye whimpered and wagged his stubtail, turning his head now toward the sound of Jeb's voice. Tears blocked Jeb's sight and he knelt beside the pup and threw his arms around its neck. The red hound whimpered again and Jeb felt the dog's body tremble. Jeb lifted the hound into his arms and ran through the willows to the path that led to the cabin. In sight of the cabin, he shouted for Grandma Quildy. And by the time he reached the yard, Grandma Quildy was out of the cabin door coming toward him.

"Jeb!" she said. "What's wrong?"

"My hound is blind," Jeb said, tears rolling down his face.

Chapter Four
THE SEARCH FOR JEPTHA
■

Grandma Quildy took the hound from Jeb's arms and took it into the cabin. She placed the red pup beside the fire grate and went quickly to the kitchen. Jeb knelt beside the pup and rubbed his hands over its red coat and spoke quietly to him. Mooneye tried once to rise to his feet but Jeb pushed him gently back to the floor. Grandma Quildy came into the room with a pan in her hands and a white cloth across her shoulder. She knelt beside the red hound and dipped the cloth into the pan of water. She gently wiped Mooneye's face. The pup flinched and whimpered and Jeb turned his head.

"He is blind, ain't he, Grandma Quildy?" Jeb said.

"I don't know," Grandma Quildy said, moving her cloth over the face of the dog, wiping away the blood.

"Jeptha would know," Jeb said. "If he were here, he would know what to do. He knew what to do for Lucy."

Grandma Quildy dipped the cloth into the pan again.

"Jeptha is not here," she said. "We will have to put our trust in the Lord. I will do all I can to help the pup."

Jeb rose to his feet and looked toward the window.

"Let me go for Jeptha," Jeb pleaded. He looked again at the red hound and his throat choked up and he couldn't speak. The hound lay trembling and flinching at the touch of the cloth.

"Jeptha is a far piece away," Grandma Quildy said. "You would be apt to lose your way. It is still dark in the trees."

"I could find my way," Jeb pleaded. "I know I could. My dog is blind, Grandma Quildy. Please let me go." Jeb wiped the tears from his eyes and tried to swallow.

Grandma Quildy looked up from the pup and studied Jeb.

"Maybe I oughtn't to let you go," she said. "It is a far piece and you will have to judge the way. Maybe I could go, but I am afraid these old legs wouldn't make the distance."

Jeb looked at Grandma Quildy. Her eyes looked as soft and tender as the white hair that touched the floor when she bent over the hound.

The Search for Jeptha

"Maybe the good Lord helps him who helps himself," she said. "Might be just sitting here is not enough. I may be wrong, Jeb, but I will tell you the way, and I will pray that the Lord will guide you."

Jeb stood at the door and waited while Grandma Quildy told him again where to find Jeptha. He was to travel the creek which would lead to the mouth of the Big Sandy River. Here he was to turn upriver. Along the edge of the banks, following the course of the river, would be a well-worn path. This would be the path that the loggers had made, riding the logs from the upper Sandy, then walking the bank back to the mill. It was an old path. Grandma Quildy's father had traveled the path long ago. And Jeptha had traveled it often. Once on the path Jeb would not get lost, but he would have to travel for almost ten miles upriver to Buchanan. Jeptha would be there.

"Watch the river, Jeb," Grandma Quildy cautioned, patting Jeb's shoulder. "It could be that the logs have been started down the river and Jeptha might pass you on the water. Stay high on the bank; the river will be swift and the bank will be soft. I will pray for you all the way, Jeb."

The red hound whined and tried to get to its feet, as if it could tell that Jeb was leaving. It sniffed the air for Jeb's scent and whined again. Jeb looked once toward the hound, and with tears in his eyes he went out the door.

Jeb walked fast through the willow grove down the creek. If Grandma Quildy was right about the path that led up river being clear of brush, he should be able to travel fast on it. The slowness on the trail would be through the willow grove and Jeb walked quickly through it to save time. Where the path was clear, he traveled without a light and followed the sound of the water. It was better than a mile to Catlettscreek but Jeb knew he would make the distance well before daylight. He passed the spot where the coon lay. Jeb thought again of Mooneye, and he wanted to run through the willows. But he knew that it would be a long way upriver on the logger's path to the mill. Grandma Quildy had told him to travel slow and save his wind and strength.

There was a change in the sound of the water from the creek. Jeb knew he was close to the river, but he could not see it. Fog had settled over the banks so thick that it was hard to see a willow tree less than a foot in front of him. The long, keen branches of the willows struck his face and stung his skin, but Jeb brushed them aside. He did not stop until he came to the end of the creek. Here

The Search for Jeptha

Jeb caught his breath and looked for the logger's path.

The fog was moving along the path like great, colored puffs of wind. Between the puffs, Jeb squinted and made out the outline of the trail. Taking a deep breath, he headed upriver.

Jeb knew that the going would be slow. The fog was so thick that in spots Jeb had to feel his way by touching the willow limbs that drooped over the path. He judged from the time that had passed since he left the cabin that it would soon be daylight. At least it would be daylight on the steep mountain tops back home where the ridge stood so tall that the fog could not climb to reach it. It seemed that he had already been walking forever. His legs began to cramp and he stopped now and then to rest. The fog was still too heavy for him to see the river, so he listened for the sound of logs upon the water. In so heavy a fog, Jeptha could slip by without his knowing and he would be gone when Jeb reached the mill.

Once Jeb heard a splash in the water and he tried to see through the fog and listened. Something was moving through the water.

"Uncle Jeptha!" Jeb hollered.

Jeb listened to his voice echoing from the other side of the river and he walked on. He walked until he became so tired that he had to stop. He braced himself against a large willow tree and breathed hard. His legs cramped harder now, and with his hand he tried to rub out the soreness. Jeb figured there was a chance that he was close to the timber mill, but there was no way to be sure. It seemed to Jeb that the fog had come to stay forever on the Big Sandy River. The hunter's horn had bounced against his side until he was sore, and if felt as heavy as a log. Jeb's hand had touched it many times as he walked the logger's path, and he had wondered why he had brought the horn with him. In his hurry, he had forgotten that it was strapped over his shoulder. Jeb's fingers ran over the curve of the horn, feeling the dampness of the fog on it, and he fingered the rawhide strap, resting upon his shoulder. And then his hand stopped. The horn, he thought. The horn might provide the way to the timber mill. Lucy was at the mill with Jeptha and, if she heard the horn, she would know that Jeb was close, and she would come to the sound. Then Jeb could follow Lucy back to the timber mill.

Jeb breathed hard and raised the horn to his lips. He blew with all his might. The deep bellow of the horn cut through the fog, drifted through the willows, and bounced along the banks of the

The Search for Jeptha

river. Jeb waited until the echo had died and then he blew again. He sat down beside the willow to wait.

The wind had moved in the willows and it blew the limbs back and forth, making a swishing sound that drifted into the hum of the river. As Jeb listened to the sound, his eyes began to close. His legs were tired, and he did not believe that he could take another step. He figured that he would rest a while.

It seemed to Jeb that he had no more than closed his eyes when something wet touched his face. At first, he thought that he had fallen asleep and rolled into the water. Then he opened his eyes and smiled.

"Lucy!" he shouted, with joy and relief.

The small redbone hound stood beside him, licking his face. She wagged her long tail and snuffed her nose into the palm of Jeb's hand. Jeb reached out his arms and hugged the old hound's neck and then he looked into the willows. He jumped to his feet.

Standing a few feet away was the biggest dog he had ever seen. It stood, its big head turned sideways, looking at Jeb with eyes as big as a butternut. Jeb looked at the broad shoulders and powerful legs. Then he looked at the short stubtail.

He smiled and reached out his hand and snapped his fingers. It was Chet Potter's bulldog—Mooneye's father.

"Come here, Stubtail," Jeb called.

The big bulldog walked over to Jeb and wagged its stubtail so fast that Jeb could hardly see it. As Jeb looked at the bulldog, he thought of how small the red hound back at the cabin would look standing beside him. Jeb patted the bulldog's head, wrapped his hand around the horn, and followed Lucy up the path.

Jeb had walked but a short distance when he saw Jeptha coming down the path to meet him.

"Jeb!" Jeptha said, frowning, "What are you doing here? Is something wrong at the cabin? Is Ma all right?"

Tears welled in Jeb's eyes.

"Mooneye is blind, Uncle Jeptha," Jeb said. "A coon did it. And you have got to come."

"We will travel by water," Jeptha said, asking no questions, and turning toward the river. "You can tell me on the way."

The next thing Jeb knew, he was stepping into a joeboat at the edge of the bank.

"Stay at the mill, Lucy," Jeb said, and he stepped into the boat and shoved it away from shore.

The boat slid into the current and headed down river. Jeb talked fast, watching Jeptha's big arms pull the oars through the water. He tried to keep his eyes open but the movement of the boat over the swift water rocked him to sleep. He did not wake up until the boat was tied at the mouth of Catlettscreek.

The fog had lifted and the path through the willows was clear. They traveled fast. Jeb walked through the yard and into the cabin behind Jeptha. Grandma Quildy was asleep in the big chair and across her feet lay the red hound. A white cloth covered his eye. As they entered the door, the pup jumped to his feet and turned toward the sound. Whining and whimpering, he made his way to the door. Grandma Quildy jumped to her feet and hugged Jeb's neck.

"God bless you, Jeb," she said. "You did make it."

She pulled up her apron and wiped her eyes.

Already Jeptha had knelt beside the red hound and had lifted the cloth.

"The Lord has blessed you, Jeb," she said. "The hound is not blind. The hide was torn above the eye and was hanging over it. It is a bad cut, but with Jeptha here to sew it up, your pup will heal."

Jeb looked at the small red hound and smiled.

The Search for Jeptha

The stubtail wagged back and forth.

"He whipped the coon in water, Uncle Jeptha," Jeb said, his chest swelling.

Jeptha removed the cloth and narrowed his eyes.

"No doubt about it, Jeb," he said, "you got yourself a coon hound."

Chapter Five
THE PROMISE
■

There were many evenings now when Jeb stood in front of the cabin and looked toward the tall ridge. Frost hovered on the grass early and the stub oaks along the slope were completely naked beneath the winter clouds. Jeb listened to the wind sing through the bare limbs of the trees, and he thought of the music of the horn that he had not blown for a long time. He could not hunt with the red hound until the cut over his eye healed. Jeb stood now in the yard and dreamed of the lonely woods. He imagined the winter-furred coon dipping his paws into the water of some creek to pull out a crawdad that was backing under a rock on the bottom of the stream. The coon moved slow and unafraid. He had scattered his trail along the ground to the stream as thick as moss on a rock, knowing that there would be no hound to trail him across the tall ridge to a tree or den.

Mooneye stood beside him. The two watched the hills. Sometimes Mooneye would throw his head into the air, sniff the wind, and whine. And then there were times that he would start for the woods and Jeb would have to call him back. He was slow to turn and always came back wagging his stubtail and whining. Jeb watched the wound over his eye closely. Each day he removed the cloth and washed the wound with poke juice that Jeptha had left for him.

During the day, Jeb worked the creek bank gathering driftwood that he stacked under the large sycamore in the cabin's yard. The hound traveled with him and sometimes, Jeb would let him trail a muskrat. This, Jeb thought, would help to keep his nose keen. Besides, muskrat usually worked for food in the cleared bottoms along the creek and here there was little or no underbrush to snag the wound, or the white bandage above the hound's eye.

Winter was sure enough in the mountains now. Jeb knew that the blue skin of the summer muskrat had changed to a deep red that would now mark it as a prime hide. Jeb set a few traps below the cabin. Mr. Tate at the feed store would be buying hides again this year and this was a way for Jeb to make money. Jeb had skinned the large coon that Mooneye had dragged from the creek and Mr. Tate had paid him two dollars for it, saying that it was the biggest coon he had ever known to be taken from the hills.

"That coon is as big as the voice of the hound," Mr. Tate told Jeb, shaking his head.

This had made Jeb happy, because he also thought that the bugle voice was bigger than all the winds of the hills.

There was no doubt, Jeb thought, the white bandage over the eye of the hound marked him as a queer-looking dog. Being white, it seemed to match the mooneye of the pup and now both eyes looked white at a distance. As Jeb looked at the white eye, he thought often of what Grandma Quildy, and even Jeptha, had told him: The good Lord takes for a reason. What he takes for a reason he will give double in return. Many evenings Jeb sat on the bank of the creek and listened to the sound of the water while he thought about what Mooneye might have been given in exchange for the eye the Lord had taken. He thought too of the men Grandma Quildy had spoken of. First there had been Samson. Samson had been given the strength to lift a mountain. Job had been given more land than you could see from the top of two mountains. Both men had been given these things because they had searched and found faith. Jeb was searching hard and he was determined to find it. So far, Grandma Quildy had not been able to find in the print of the Book anything that said a hound-dog might have faith, so Jeb thought that he must find faith for himself and the pup, too. Jeb knew this would be a lot of faith, but he loved the red hound more than almost anything and he wanted more than anything to help take away the hound's blindness, so that people would not laugh when they saw him. The stubtail was not nearly so bad now that Jeb had seen the great bulldog. No one laughed at the bulldog, Jeb thought. They were afraid to.

The more Jeb thought about the eye, the more he believed that his hound would be given something in exchange for it. Not long ago he had asked Grandma Quildy about it and she had said:

"You just keep searching and finding faith, Jeb. And whatever the good Lord intends will come."

There had been times when Jeb thought he would not have the patience of Job. He had become restless, and he mentioned it again to Grandma Quildy. Once again she told him:

"The Lord is a busy man, Jeb. Winter is here now and there is a lot of work for Him to do. He will have to sprinkle snow over the mountains before long. Once the snow is on the ground, He will have to provide food for all the birds and the animals of the hills. Winter is a busy time. It is not like summer when there is feed in the fields. But I reckon He ain't forgot that there is a mooneyed hound down here, or a boy searching for faith. When the snow comes He remembers even the little sparrow that you see hovered in the limbs of the sycamore here in the yard. Here and there He patches the snow and leaves the ground open for the sparrow to scratch for food. You know if He can remember as little a thing as a sparrow that He will remember you and your hound."

Jeb worked around the cabin and waited.

Chapter Six
A TRAIL OF FAITH
■

When the weekend came, Jeb went to the store to buy supplies for Grandma Quildy. Several men sat around the pot-bellied stove in the middle of Mr. Tate's feed store. While Mr. Tate filled Jeb's order, Jeb listened to the men talk. Now and then Mr. Tate stopped to join in. The men spoke of coon. They discussed a great contest that was soon to be held somewhere down river to judge the best coon hound in the state of Kentucky. Mooneye stood at the edge of the door watching Jeb, and one of the men saw him.

"Maybe Jeb could enter the bobtailed hound," he said, pointing with his finger toward the door. All of the men looked and laughed. "I reckon, though, it would take better than a mooneyed hound to win a state championship," he added.

Jeb looked at Mooneye. The stubtail wagged back and forth and he cocked his head to one side and looked at the man that had spoken his name. And then he looked back at Jeb.

"One thing in his favor," another of the men

said. "He wouldn't have the tail to slow him down."

They all laughed again. Jeb frowned and lowered his eyes to the floor. He had become used to men laughing at the hound's mooneye and stubtail, but it still made him angry. Once he would have been quick to tell them of the red dog's bugle voice, and of the large coon he had killed in water. He could tell them that it was not the white eye or stubtail that filled the dark woods with hunting music, or gave the hound a keen nose. But Jeb had learned that to tell them was to only bring more laughter.

"I wouldn't be so fast to judge against the red hound," Mr. Tate said, looking toward Jeb. "Maybe you know dogs better than me, but this much I know: ain't a man here that don't know the dog's mother, Lucy. She is old now, but each of you has seen the day when she run your hounds ragged. I say the pup here is better than Lucy."

"Reckon that's like you, Tate," Bunt Borders, the fox hunter, said, grinning. "You got to watch business. But just because the customer is always right don't mean his hound is." Jeb watched Bunt Borders kick his legs in the air; rear back on the bench and laugh. The other men on the bench joined in. That is, all the men but Mr. Tate. He looked at Jeb with a kind smile on his face.

Jeb was always anxious to get his order and go back over the mountain. In the hills and at the cabin, there was never anyone to laugh at the red hound. And yet today, even though men laughed at the hound, Jeb was hoping that Mr. Tate would take longer to fill the order. The men had turned back to talking and Jeb strained to listen. It was not often that Jeb got to listen to men talk of coon hunting. There was only the times that Jeptha was at the cabin.

Coon talk, said Grandma Quildy, was men talk.

Jeb listened closely while the men talked about the championship race. There would be as many as fifteen hounds running at one time. And these hounds would be the best that could be found. They would be wise and well-trained hounds that had pushed more coon to the tree than Jeb could ever hope to see. The hounds would follow a manmade coon trail, tracking for close to three miles to reach the end where a live coon would be tied in a tree. The hound that could follow the trail and lead the pack and go on to tree the coon would win the championship and become the best coon hound in the whole state of Kentucky. Jeb did not know how big the state was, but Jeptha had told him that it was bordered by the great

A Trail of Faith

Ohio River, and you could travel the river for days without coming to the end of it. The valley where Jeb lived was only part of the state. Perhaps it was like a small seed in a great field. This was something Grandma Quildy had told Jeb during one of the school lessons that she gave him.

Jeb's eyes grew big. And as he listened to the tales of the contest, he could imagine his red hound leading the pack, coming in to the tree that held the coon. No one would laugh at the mooneye or stubtail of the hound when they heard the bugle voice that would make him the greatest coon dog in the whole state of Kentucky.

Jeb raised his eyes and frowned. The race would be held far away—perhaps a day's travel down river. A man would have to pay to enter his hound, and he would have to send word that he was coming. And there was little time left.

Jeb took the sack from Mr. Tate and walked out the door. The hound ran up the path, stopped, and waited for Jeb to climb the ridge. Jeb stood in the path. The pup whimpered and waited. Then it turned and ran down the path to where Jeb stood. Jeb walked slowly over the clay path and looked back toward the store. The pup ran ahead and cut into the woods to sniff for a trail. Jeb did not notice. His mind was far away, down river. He was standing again at the tree. Around Mooneye's neck, he imagined the blue ribbon that the winning hound would wear. Other hunters were bragging on the red hound and not one was laughing.

    Jeb raised his eyes and looked toward the ridge. Could the trip down river be the trail that he was to follow in his search for faith? Could this be the promise? Jeb kicked at the red clay and turned up the path.

Chapter Seven
A TOUCH OF FAITH
■

As he gathered an armload of driftwood along the creek, Jeb could not forget the talk he had heard at Mr. Tate's store. When he closed his eyes, he was in a strange country. The bottoms along the creek reminded him of the open field the hounds would break across at the race as they came toward the tree. The willows to Jeb were the woods where the trail would begin. And each time the pup came through the willows sniffing the ground, Jeb's heart beat fast and his chest swelled with pride. Now and then he stopped and looked toward the top of the steep ridge, watching the evening sun that hovered like a red bird trying to roost on top of the tallest black oak on the ridge.

Finally Jeb laid the armload of wood on the ground and called his hound.

"Maybe," he said, "we can make it to Mr. Tate's store before the sun sets."

Jeb started down the willow path toward the trail that would lead over the ridge to the store.

The Mooneyed Hound

Now and then he stopped to call the red hound, who was sniffing into every brush pile. On top of the ridge, Jeb stopped and called the pup.

"Mooneye," he said, looking toward the sky. "This is no time for trailing. We have got to hurry. Now, stay on the path."

The hound lowered its eyes and trotted beside Jeb down the other side of the ridge to the store.

Luck was with him, Jeb thought, walking inside the door and eyeing the empty bench. Mr. Tate was at the end of the large oak counter weighing feed from a barrel and placing large scoops in paper sacks. Mr. Tate looked up at Jeb and smiled.

"Well, Jeb," he said, "forget something the last trip?"

Jeb moved uneasily and looked around the store.

"No," he said.

"Well, then," Mr. Tate said. "Reckon you came to talk."

"I came to ask a question," Jeb said.

Mr. Tate placed the scoop on the counter and looked carefully at Jeb.

"Must be a mighty important question for you to come all the way over the ridge with the shadows as close to the trees as they are," Mr.

Tate said. "Don't reckon darkness bothers a hunter, though. What is this question, Jeb?"

Jeb hesitated for a minute and then caught his breath. He spoke to Mr. Tate with a worried look on his face.

"Could a mooneyed hound run in the state championship?" Jeb asked.

Mr. Tate rubbed his chin and looked at Jeb out of the corner of his eyes.

"You mean your mooneyed hound, Jeb?" Mr. Tate asked.

Mooneye looked at Mr. Tate and wagged his stubtail.

"I reckon I mean just a mooneyed hound," Jeb said, hoping that Mr. Tate would not know what he was thinking.

Mr. Tate looked at the red hound and then back at Jeb. He frowned and there were deep wrinkles in his face, same as there were in Grandma Quildy's face. Mr. Tate had lived long in the hills, too.

"Well," he said. "I reckon if a man was to have a mooneyed hound, he could sure enough enter. Providing it was a coon dog. It ain't just an ordinary race, Jeb. This race is for the best of the best hounds."

"If a hound had no tail to swish," Jeb said,

"could he still run?" Jeb looked toward the potbellied stove.

"Reckon he could," Mr. Tate said. "Man don't have no power to change the look of a hound, Jeb. Things such as that are the work of the Lord. No hunter will go against it. And only fool people laugh if a dog is not pretty. It is a hound with a keen nose and a master that believes in that keen nose that makes a champion."

Jeb was so happy that he could have hugged Mr. Tate's neck. Mr. Tate was a good man, and he must have searched for faith to believe what he had said.

"Would it take long to travel to the race?" Jeb asked, then quickly added: "If someone was planning to go."

Mr. Tate looked at Jeb.

"Reckon if he went by water it wouldn't take too long," Mr. Tate said.

Jeb caught his breath.

"If a man's hound was to win, nobody would laugh at the hound then, would they, Mr. Tate?" Jeb said.

"I should reckon not," Mr. Tate said. "No one laughs at a champion. And only fools laugh at a loser. He would probably be a great dog if he was even entered in the race."

A Touch of Faith

Mr. Tate walked to the end of the counter and picked up a white envelope. He fumbled with the envelope and then pulled out a white sheet of paper.

"Maybe this will answer your question, Jeb." he said, holding out the paper. "This is the contest rules and the entry blank that a man would have to have if he was fixing to go."

Jeb took the paper. His heart beat fast as he read:

30th Annual
KENTUCKY CHAMPIONSHIP
Coon Dog Field Trial

Leafy Oak Farm
OAKPORT, KENTUCKY
Saturday, November 20
First Tree
Entry Fee--$10.00
Winner--$75.00
Entries Close November 15

Mail Entries To
Zack Hewlett
Kentucky Championship Coon Dog Trial
Oakport, Kentucky

Jeb caught his breath when he saw the seventy-five dollars that would be given to the winning hound. It was more money than he figured he would see in a lifetime. And then he looked at the ten dollar entry fee. He also knew that ten dollars was more money than he had ever earned at one time. And there was so little time to earn it. He had the two dollars Mr. Tate had given him for the coonskin, he thought, and there were three muskrat hides drying at the cabin.

"Ten dollars is a lot of money, ain't it, Mr. Tate?" Jeb said, looking away from the letter.

"Reckon it wouldn't be too much if a man was determined to get it," Mr. Tate said. "He would have all kinds of chances--if he knew the hills, that is. Furs will bring a good price this year. Herb roots will be high. I could even use some sweet anise root if I could buy them. If a man was to know the woods, I'd say he'd make it."

The frown left Jeb's face and he smiled. Jeb was not a stranger to the hills. He knew that mayapple and ginseng herb roots grew in the hollows where the shade of the trees kept the ground rich and soft. Sweet anise could be found a little higher on the slope, but still under the shade of the trees. The soft mud of the creek bank held the sign of the muskrat and told a hunter where to place his trap.

"Meant to tell you this morning, Jeb," Mr. Tate said. "Slipped my mind though. I'll be needing a cord of wood right away. Jeptha says that you are a good man with an ax."

Tears welled in Jeb's eyes, he was so happy. He scanned the paper again and handed it back to Mr. Tate. The sun had set below the ridge and it would soon be dark. Grandma Quildy would be worried.

"Why don't you keep the letter and entry blank, Jeb," Mr. Tate said. "Old man like me with no hound has got no use for it. Might be you know someone who might want to use it." He looked at Jeb and winked his eye.

Jeb folded the letter, smiled at Mr. Tate, and hurried out the door. A short distance up the path he heard Mr. Tate holler and he stopped and turned.

"Bring me the entry blank when you have filled it out, Jeb," Mr. Tate called, "and I'll give it to the mail carrier."

Jeb caught his breath, then turned up the path. Mr. Tate had known all the time, he thought. Jeb stopped and turned back toward the feed store. Mr. Tate walked out to meet him.

The Mooneyed Hound

"You won't tell anyone, will you, Mr. Tate?" Jeb said. He could just see the men gathered around the potbellied stove laughing at his plan.

"Tell you what," Mr. Tate said. "It will be a secret between you and me and the mooneyed hound." He shook his head and chuckled. "What I'd give to see that mooneyed hound win. I'd get rid of the store loafers then, I'll bet." He laughed out loud and patted Jeb on the shoulder. "Lord be with you, Jeb."

Jeb hurried up the path. The shadows moved through the trees and it would be dark soon.

Chapter Eight
THE ENTRY
■

That night, after dark, Jeb sneaked out the letter and, holding it up to the light of the moon that sifted in through the window, he read it again. He took the two dollars that he had gotten from Mr. Tate for the coonskin, folded them up in the letter, and hid the letter under the eaves of he cabin roof. In two weeks he knew that he would have to earn eight more dollars. The muskrat hides that he had at the cabin would bring maybe two more dollars. If so, that would make four. And all of the money, Jeb thought, would come from the hills.

He felt good knowing the mountains he loved so much had provided him with a way to make money. Tomorrow he would go to the hollow and gather herb roots, and the next day he would cut wood for Mr. Tate. When he was sure that he could get the money he would write the letter and fill out the entry. The entry fee money would not have to be sent, but would have to be paid at the race. Jeb listened to the sparrows chatter under the eaves of the roof. He slipped under the covers. He lay there listening to the sparrows again and he thought of what Grandma Quildy had said about the Lord not forgetting the little sparrow. Somehow he felt that the Lord had not forgotten him, and that He was now providing a way. It seemed funny to him, but in a way he felt akin to the little sparrow that hovered in the sycamore in the winter months.

At daylight Jeb was at the creek. The traps he had set held two more rats. One of the rats was small and was known as a kit. It would not bring much. But the other was a large brown rat and might bring enough to make up for the small one. The red hound watched Jeb as he took the rats from the traps and carried them to the bank. He sniffed the rats with his nose and then wagged his stubtail back and forth. The wound over his eye had healed enough so that Jeb had taken off the white bandage. The wound had not affected his eye and the red hound was quick to catch the sight of anything that moved. And he had worked too, Jeb thought. He had trailed the muskrat, helping Jeb to find places to set the traps.

Jeb skinned the rats on the bank and then turned into the hollow to gather herb roots. Under the shade of a beech tree, he found a bunch of

mayapple and with his knife he dug under the tender roots. Higher on the bluff, under the shade of hickory and slick-barked poplar trees, he found sweet anise. The sweet anise roots grew deep and Jeb had to dig carefully and deep so that he would not break the root. The hound sat on the slope, eyeing Jeb and cocking his head to one side, watching the hole where Jeb dug like he expected something to run out of it.

Jeb looked at the red hound and smiled. He was determined now to go to the race. He had worked hard to earn the money for the entry fee. He did not know yet how he would get there. He knew that it was a far piece away and a strange country to him. But it would not be strange country to Jeptha, Jeb thought. Jeptha had traveled the river, as much as he had traveled the hills. And so, on the broad shoulders of Jeptha rested Jeb's chance. Jeb did not know how he would get Jeptha to take him. He would have to plan a way. And this would perhaps be the hardest part of Jeb's plan, so he saved it till last. But time was passing fast. As it was, Jeptha did not even know that Jeb wanted to go to the race. No one knew but Mr. Tate. But there was one more person, Jeb thought, and he turned his eyes toward the clouds. The Lord knew everything, according to

The Entry

Grandma Quildy. So He knew what Jeb was planning to do. In fact, Jeb thought, if he had the faith of Job, the Lord might even lead the way, and the country would not be strange to Him.

Jeb had searched for faith. He had helped Grandma Quildy in every way he could and in a way, he thought, he had even helped the Lord. He had broken bread into crumbs and fed the sparrows. Jeb believed with all his heart in the red hound and, according to Mr. Tate, this was what it took to win.

After Jeb cut the wood for Mr. Tate, he counted his money. And in the folded sheet of paper he had nine dollars. Two muskrat hides hung from the side of the shed and would make him ten dollars. On the bank of the creek, Jeb sat down and wrote a letter.

Dear Zack Hewlett,

My name is Jeb Lockwood and I live in the Big Sandy Valley. I have a hound-dog here that is named Mooneye. He has a white eye that Uncle Jeptha says is a true mark of the moon and he also has a stubtail. He is a good coon dog and is broke to the horn. I have earned my ten dollars and will bring it with me to enter Mooneye in the state championship. Mr. Tate will give this letter

to the mail carrier that comes by his store once a week.
Jeb Lockwood
Big Sandy Valley, Ky.

    Jeb looked at the letter and his chest swelled with pride. He could remember the many evenings that he had been forced to sit in the cabin while Grandma Quildy told him that he must learn to read and write. He had squirmed and listened to the wind in the sycamore outside and watched the sun through the window. Using the print from the Bible, Grandma Quildy had scratched down the words that Jeb had followed with pain. And while he learned to write the words, he had listened to Grandma Quildy as she spoke of a day when he would be putting on paper what he wanted to say and sending his thoughts farther than the voice could ever travel. He had not believed her then. But that time had now come. And Jeb wished now that he had watched and listened closer. Maybe he wouldn't have had to copy some of the words from the entry letter in order to spell them.
    Jeb folded the letter and looked toward the moon that circled the ridge. Beyond this moon lived the Man that was watching him search for

The Entry

faith. And beyond this Moon was the Man who would send a gift to the mooneyed hound.

"Lord," Jeb said, "I reckon that I have searched as hard as I know how. The rest is up to You, Jeptha, and Grandma Quildy. Me and Mooneye are ready. If You could show Grandma Quildy something in the Book that might say we can go, I sure would be obliged to You. I don't believe she cares a lot about hound talk, but Uncle Jeptha will take me if she says so. I'm asking Your help. Amen."

Jeb looked at the hunter's horn that lay beside his bed. Mooneye was too big now to curl up in the curve of the horn. He was no longer a pup. He was a hound. And he was the greatest hound in the world, Jeb thought.

Chapter Nine
THE SECRET
■

There was a heavy frost on the ground as Jeb followed the path to the feed store. As he turned out the door to cross the ridge back to the cabin, he could still see the tracks that he had made coming down the slope. He had watched Mr. Tate seal the envelope with his letter in it and place it on the stack with others that he had to mail. Jeb felt good knowing that his letter had been placed on top and he thought of the long journey it would make. It seemed a great thing. Here he was up in the Big Sandy Valley telling a man down in Oakport, Kentucky, that he was bringing his mooneyed hound there to chase a coon.

He had been able to do this only because Grandma Quildy had taught him to write. Grandma Quildy was old, Jeb thought, but she was smart. She was the smartest person Jeb knew. Jeptha was smart, but it had been Grandma Quildy who had taught him most all he knew. Jeptha, he figured, knew many things, but Grandma Quildy knew almost all things. She knew the woods as well as a hunter. She had even killed a wildcat. She could read and she could write. She knew where the ginseng and mayapple roots grew. In fact, she had taught Jeb where they were. She had showed him how they were used as medicine, and more than once Jeb had carried the medicine from it to a sick neighbor. She was powerful enough to cut into a four-inch sapling with one swing of an ax, yet tender enough to mend the broken wing of a sparrow. Although the skin around her eyes was now wrinkled, they were still keen. They knew where to look for faith and how to find the answer to problems in the print of the Book. Grandma Quildy never lost faith. It was she who had once believed in the red hound even when Jeb had doubted. At first, Jeb had been ashamed of the mooneye and stubtail of the hound. It was Grandma Quildy who had taught him to love it.

She had taught him to love many things here in the mountains that he had once laughed at. They were the things that Jeb thought had been shunned and he had not bothered to look for their purpose. There was the scrub oak that stood on the side of a red clay slope. The scrub oak was an ugly tree and looked useless and puny beside the tall black oak on the ridge. And yet it was the roots of the scrub oak that bound the clay on the slope and held it so that it could not roll off the slope and cover the rich black loam of the valley that was used for gardens. And then, there was the locust tree. Small thorns covered the bark of locust and it was no good for shade. Birds seldom lit on the bare limbs. The small, white blooms that came to the tree in May disappeared with a puff of wind leaving the long, skimpy-leafed limbs that could not hold back the sun like the broad leaf of the sugar maple. And yet, stretched around the rugged mountain farms holding wire so the cattle could not stray were the strong trunks of the locust. Locust posts could stand in the ground, it seemed, as long as time itself, and the winds and rain that weakened and rotted other trees could not dent the locust.

And then there was the red hound. The white eye and stubtail marked it from all other hounds of the mountains. People laughed at it as Jeb had once laughed at the ugly trees. Since Jeb had learned the purpose of the trees, they no longer seemed ugly as he passed them on the hill. There was a purpose, too, he thought, for the mooneye and stubtail of the hound. And once people learned what it was they would not laugh anymore.

Jeb was always wondering what the purpose

The Secret

might be. But he did not question the reasoning of the Lord. He was going to wait and be patient like Job had been. But if Jeb could have asked for the gift, he would have asked for the red hound to win the championship. One day it would come, he thought, and then he would know.

Jeb felt confident. He was filled with determination when he crossed the ridge to the cabin. Anytime now, he figured, Grandma Quildy was apt to run across print in her Book that would say that Jeb should go. This was what Jeb had asked, and he had the faith that it would happen. But just in case it didn't, he also had another plan. Jeptha would be coming any day now and Jeb figured that he would walk up to him and, like a man, he would ask Jeptha to take him to Oakport. Sitting at the cabin to wait might not be enough, he figured. Grandma Quildy had said that the Lord would help those that helped themselves. She had let him go up Sandy to find Jeptha the night the hound had been cut by the coon. If Jeptha would not take him, he would have to ask Grandma Quildy if he could go alone.

Grandma Quildy was standing in the yard as Jeb walked out of the willow grove. From the edge of the yard, Jeb could see that she was holding something in her hand. He squinted and looked again. And then he caught his breath. In her hand was a folded paper with his money in it. He had taken out the entry blank and mailed it, but back under the eaves he had placed the money wrapped in the contest rules.

"Come to the cabin, Jeb," she said. "I want to talk to you."

Jeb lowered his head and walked into the cabin. The last thing he had intended was to tell Grandma Quildy. He had thought that by this time she would have found what he wanted her to find in the print of the Book. But now he wondered if the print might have told her that he had money hid under the eaves.

Grandma Quildy sat down in the chair by the fire and opened the letter. She squinted her eyes as she read and she counted the money.

"This is a lot of money, Jeb," she said. "You have surely worked hard to earn it."

She looked at the letter again squinting, Jeb thought, at several of the larger words and then she looked up again.

"You have been keeping this a secret from your old Granny, ain't you, Jeb?" she said. "You didn't need to. You don't ever need to hide things from me. I knew that the letter and the money was there all the time. And I have been watching the

The Secret

money grow. I been praying, too, that you would make it. You are a fine worker, and you have surely had a lot of faith. To earn ten dollars is to earn a lot of money. Is this what you want to use it for, Jeb?"

Jeb was almost too surprised now to answer Grandma Quildy. For many days now he had sneaked the money to his room and hid it, or thought he was hiding it. There had been days when he had wanted so much to come to her and show her the money he had earned. But then he would have had to tell her about the championship race, and he wanted to prove to her that he could earn the money it would cost to enter. He looked at Grandma Quildy and rubbed his eyes.

"I want more than anything else to enter my hound in the championship race," he said.

"I might have known," Grandma Quildy said, grinning now for the first time, and shaking her head. "You are just like your Uncle Jeptha. There is little before your eyes except the tall trees, the dark woods, and a hound-dog. It is a good life, though, I reckon. It is honest and not to be ashamed of."

Jeb took a deep breath. He felt proud that Grandma Quildy had said he was like Jeptha. Jeptha was the smartest man in the mountains.

He knew more about a hound-dog than anyone else. And he knew the trails of the woods so well that he could walk them on the darkest night without a flashlight.

Grandma Quildy was looking at the paper again. She frowned and spoke:

"Many years ago," she said, "when Jeptha was about your age, he had a hound-dog. It was the first hound he ever owned and he named it Sermon. I think he named it this because he had found out that this name was in the print of the Bible and he wanted to get on the good side of me, knowing I didn't care a lot for hound-dogs. He trained that hound night and day, and they became as close to one another as the bark to a tree. One day I heard him speak to his Pa about taking him down the Ohio to enter his hound in the same race. Jeptha knew that his Pa knew the river and had been a hound-dog man all his life. I was against his going. It was a long distance, and I knew I would be left alone at the cabin. His Pa went against me and offered to take him. Two days before he was to go, Sermon was bit by a rattlesnake and died the same night. I had never known until then that the hound had meant so much to Jeptha, and in some way I felt guilty that the hound had died. Jeptha had never thought I cared

The Secret

much for his hound. He never knew of the many days I had fed it without his knowing. He seemed to think that I had been against the hound. 'Ma,' he says, 'one day I will own another hound, and I will take it to the championship and I will be the first boy in the Big Sandy Valley to own the best coon dog in the whole state.' Your Grandpa died and Jeptha had to take his place at the timber mill. He didn't forget the race, though, and for years he often spoke of it. He never stopped dreaming about it. But I think that he felt I didn't want him to go, because he had to make a living here for the cabin. So one day he quit talking about it. He held a man's job in the tall timbers." Grandma Quildy looked out the window toward the tall trees of the hills. "He never knew all the times I prayed for him. One day you will go, Jeptha, I hoped." She turned then and looked straight at Jeb.

"What makes you want to go, Jeb?" she asked.

"I want my hound to win," Jeb said.

"Winning the race will not make the hound a better hunter, Jeb," she said. "Ten dollars is a lot of money to enter. There is a greater reason, ain't there, Jeb?"

"I figured," Jeb said, catching his breath, "if Mooneye could win the race no one would laugh at him again. And then all the little mooneyed pups that the Lord pushes out of the clouds and sets on the mountains like you say He does will not ever have to worry about people laughing at them either. Because they will know that Mooneye was a white-eyed hound and was the greatest coon hound in the whole state of Kentucky."

Grandma Quildy looked at Jeb with love in her eyes.

"But it is a big race, Jeb," she said. "There will be a lot of hounds there. Maybe Mooneye won't win."

"He will win," Jeb said, drawing up his lip. "I know he will. The Lord has promised Mooneye something, because he set him on the mountain with a blind eye, and I believe it will be that he wins the race."

Grandma Quildy frowned.

"How do you know that winning the race will be what the Lord intended?" she said.

Jeb studied a while and then looked straight at Grandma Quildy.

"Because I have got faith," Jeb said. "Do you reckon Jeptha will take me?"

Grandma Quildy wiped her face with her apron.

"Tell me this, Jeb," she asked. "Say you did

The Secret

go. But say that Mooneye didn't win. Another hound comes in ahead of him. No matter how you might feel, would you remember that it might not be what the Lord intended? To show that you are not mad, would you be willing to pray for the winner and his hound?"

Jeb frowned. He thought of another hound pushing to the tree ahead of Mooneye. It would be hard to pray for a dog that beat his hound. But he remembered how Samson had prayed for all the people that had laughed at him, and so had Job.

"Yes, I would," Jeb said.

"Then, about Jeptha," she said. "I have prayed that one day he would get to go. I even thought once that maybe he would take Lucy. But I know now she is an old hound, just as I am an old woman. Neither are of much use, I reckon. I reckon too, a man with your faith would have to go, wouldn't he?"

"Lucy is a great hound," Jeb said, "and you, Grandma Quildy, are the greatest person in the whole world."

Jeb threw his arms around Grandma Quildy's neck and he could feel the tears on her cheeks.

Chapter Ten
JEPTHA FINDS A WAY
■

With Grandma Quildy's faith added to his, Jeb went around the house happier than he had ever been in his whole life. Jeptha had come to the cabin, and there had been but little coaxing on Grandma Quildy's part for Jeptha to agree to make the trip down river. In fact, it seemed to Jeb that Jeptha thought it was he who was entering the red hound instead of Jeb. He humored the mooneyed hound more than Jeb, and it wasn't long before even Lucy let him know it. The old hound stood with her head low and her eyes fixed on Jeptha watching him humor the pup.

The second day Jeptha was at the cabin, he took some coon scent and dragged it through the tall trees and fixed it on a large oak on top of the ridge. Then he set the red hound on the trail and watched the pup work it to the tree.

"Best nose I ever seen on a hound," he said, listening to the bugle voice drift back down the slope.

The Mooneyed Hound

He would not let Lucy work the trail with Mooneye, afraid that she might bother him on the scent. But when Lucy heard the mooneyed hound bark treed, she lifted her head into the air and bawled and started to break for the tree. Jeptha spoke and the old hound wagged her tail and walked slowly back beside him. Jeptha looked at the old hound with soft eyes and motioned her toward the tree. She moved up the slope and before long her voice joined that of the red hound.

"Lucy is the greatest hound I ever owned, Jeb," Jeptha said. "I believe she could have won the state championship once. Now she is an old hound. She is steady but too slow on the trail for a fast race. But she has given many things to Mooneye. She has given him her keen nose, and her bugle voice, and the heart of a great hound; it will take all of these to win. Listen to their bark. One is from an old hound and one is from a young, that is the only difference."

Grandma Quildy had become quiet since Jeptha had come. She had very little to say. After her work was done at the cabin, she spent her time sitting in her chair by the fire reading the Bible. Jeb watched her and he often wished that she might be praying that the hound might be

Jeptha Finds a Way

guided along the coon trail like she had often prayed for Jeptha to be guided along the tramroads.

A day before the race, Jeptha left the cabin and headed for town. He would be searching for a way down the Ohio, he said. And Jeb sat under the willows with the red hound and Lucy beside him, and they all three watched the willow path. With every movement of the brush, Jeb jumped with the hounds. It was close to dark before Jeptha came up the path. He grinned and stooped and ran his large hand over the head of the old hound, and then he looked at Jeb.

"Reckon we ought to be packing, Jeb," he said, "we will be leaving before daylight in the morning. A logging friend of mine who is the captain of the paddle-wheel boat, <u>Sandy Shoal</u>, is taking a run of logs below Oakport in the morning. According to him, he has got just enough room left for two men and a hound-dog."

Jeb could hardly wait to tell Grandma Quildy the good news. He ran to the cabin, and he talked so fast she had to slow him down. She watched him with a smile on her face and then she lowered her head.

"It is a far piece, Jeb," she said. "I will miss you here at the cabin. I will worry, too. You might get down there and forget to come back to your old Grandma."

Jeb looked at the gray hair and wrinkled face.

"Uncle Jeptha says that the boat will be coming back to the Big Sandy River after the race tomorrow," Jeb said. "As soon as Mooneye wins the race, I will get back on the boat and come home."

"I reckon," Grandma Quildy said, "I can watch the willow path for you."

It seemed to Jeb that the night would never end. He tossed in his bed and glanced out the window and looked toward the steep ridge. He thought of the big boat that he would ride down the Ohio River. And he thought of the great coon race. Once he looked beside his bed where the red hound was supposed to be sleeping. The hound's eyes were wide open and he stared back at Jeb, the stubtail making a thumping noise against the floor.

"You better close your eyes, Mooneye," Jeb said. "You got a long trail tomorrow and a lot of hounds to beat."

The hound closed his eyes and Jeb listened to the stubtail still thumping.

Chapter Eleven
THE STUBLEG CAPTAIN
■

Daylight had not seeped over the ridge, but the morning wind was in the sycamore limbs. Jeb felt the bed shake and, thinking the red hound had jumped up in it, he started to scold him. But when he opened his eyes he saw that it was not Mooneye. Jeptha stood over the bed, dressed and smiling.

"Don't reckon you was ever woke before daylight to go on a coon hunt, was you?" Jeptha said. "Better hurry. We got to be at the river after the light comes down. And your Grandma won't let you go before you eat." Jeptha glanced toward the window and then spoke to the red hound that stood sniffing and whining at his feet.

Jeb rolled in the bed and squinted his eyes.

"Fact is," Jeptha said, "if we don't get away from here before long she might change her mind. Reckon she is afraid you might see the river and take a liking to it like me and Pa."

Jeb jumped out of bed and pulled on his shoes. He brushed his hair out of his eyes and walked with Jeptha to the kitchen. Grandma

Quildy scolded him twice for eating too fast. Then Jeb dressed for the trip. Mooneye was fed a good meal and this meal, according to Jeptha, would be the last he would get until the race was over. Lucy stayed close to Jeptha's feet and watched his every move with her sad eyes. She watched the red hound, too, wagging her long tail when she caught his eyes. Mooneye wagged his stubtail back and forth. He cocked his head to one side and watched Jeb sling the strap of the hunter's horn over his shoulder. And then he whined and jumped up and down.

Jeb stood in the yard and listened again while Grandma Quildy cautioned him about the water. And then she looked at him for a minute and reached out and hugged his neck.

"God bless you, Jeb," she said. "And God bless your mooneyed hound. Take care of them, Jeptha."

Jeptha nodded his head and turned down the path. Lucy wagged her long tail and started toward him. Jeptha stopped.

"Sorry, Lucy," he said. "I reckon you got to stay here with Ma and help look after her."

Lucy wagged her long tail in the clay dust and turned back toward the cabin, as if she had understood what Jeptha had said. Jeb looked back along the willow path and waved at Grandma

The Stubleg Captain

Quildy. The old hound stood beside her, looking down the path.

Light had crossed the ridge when Jeb and Jeptha stepped out of the hollow and onto the brick road of the town. Jeb stopped long enough to slip a rope around Mooneye's neck and lead him across town. This would be strange country to the hound, and Jeb did not want him to stray. Mooneye jerked and pulled at the rope and looked at Jeb with sad eyes as if he thought he was being punished for something he had done. Jeptha paid no attention to them and Jeb had to walk fast to stay beside him.

They walked across the small town of Catlettsville. Dried river mud covered the brick streets of the town and the old buildings looked as quiet as the gray rocks of the hills. A dim light seeped over the ridge in back of the town and spread over the brick road. Jeptha walked toward the river. Two men stood near the water's edge. Jeb saw one of them point with his finger toward the red hound. The other man looked and Jeb could see a grin on his face. Jeb walked on, leading Mooneye.

At the edge of town Jeb stood and looked out over two rivers. One river was the broad Ohio, which he would travel. The smaller river was the Big Sandy. The small river was jutted with many sandbars. On the far side, an arrow-shaped piece of land guided the water into the Ohio. The land that shaped the arrow was in West Virginia, the home of the great bulldog, father of Mooneye. Willow saplings grew thick down the bank to the edge of the water. Over the top of them, Jeb saw the boat. The great paddle wheel on the back turned around and around and churned the water into white foam that looked like puffs of white clouds. The paddle wheel was pulling the boat closer to a long tow of logs that had been rafted together. Men stood on the edge of the boat and on the logs throwing and catching ropes and tying them. Jeb walked behind Jeptha down the bank to the edge of the water.

"Howdy, Peg," Jeptha squinted and waved at a man standing inside a cabin raised high on the front of the boat.

The captain looked toward Jeptha and waved back. He leaned his head out a small window and hollered:

"Be putting to shore in a minute. Quick as I get my logs tied."

Jeptha waved again and Jeb stood beside him and looked across the water. Mooneye cocked his head and watched the great wheel turn. He whined and jumped toward it and then hunkered

and stuck his head into Jeb's hands.

The boat pulled into shore and two men stretched a board to the bank. Jeptha walked the plank and looked back at Jeb. The men on the boat watched Jeb lead the hound across the board. Mooneye walked carefully. On the deck, Jeb spoke to the men as Jeptha called their names and he watched closely as one of the men stooped beside Mooneye. Jeb watched the man rub his hand over the chest of the hound and then let it slide across Mooneye's broad head.

"He's a lot of hound," he finally said. "Looks like old Lucy herself. Blind in one eye, ain't he? Stubtailed too, like that bulldog of Chet Potter's." Jeb saw him grin.

Jeb caught his breath and started to answer the man, telling him of the bugle voice and of the coon that he had whipped in water. Someone hollered his name.

"Up here, Jeb," he said. "Bring your hound and come up."

Jeb turned his head and saw the captain leaning out the window. He was smiling and waving his hand, motioning Jeb up the wooden ladder that led to the small cabin. Jeb carried the red hound up the ladder into the pilothouse.

Captain Peg stood at the wheel guiding the

The Stubleg Captain

boat. From the shore, he had looked like a big man. But he was little, smaller than any of the crew. He kept his hands on the wheel and turned and faced Jeb. Jeb could see that he stood on one leg. The right leg was gone and there was a wooden stub in its place. Jeb jerked his head and hoped that Captain Peg had not caught him staring at his wooden leg.

"Look over the water, Jeb," he said. "You can see almost as far as you can from the top of a mountain."

Jeb looked out over the water. It looked like a long blue path of clouds. But the path did not weave through black oak and shellbark hickory like a cloud, it twisted through willows, sugar maple, and here and there the white-barked water birch.

Jeb watched and listened to Captain Peg talk of the river. Now and then he turned his head to watch the paddle wheel churn the water. Jeb caught Captain Peg staring at the red hound and he wondered if he was noticing the mooneye and stubtail.

"Lot of hound there," Captain Peg said, reaching down to pet the red hound. "Believe he likes me, too. Maybe it's because me and this hound have something in common. He's got a stubtail and I got a stubleg." Captain Peg looked at Jeb and grinned. And for the first time Jeb grinned back at a man who had said something about the stubtail or white eye of his hound.

"Ain't nothing wrong with a stubtail though," Captain Peg said. "No, sir, nothing at all. Nothing wrong with a stubleg either. I used to think there might be back when I first lost the leg falling into the paddle wheel. Thought I wouldn't be able to follow the river anymore." Captain Peg looked across the water and shook his head. "Funny thing; when I had two good legs I couldn't learn a thing. Couldn't hardly remember where the river emptied, let alone where the shoals and snags were. A captain has got to know these things. I was just a deckhand back then. But after I lost the leg, my eyes became sharper. I got to where I could spot the bark on a willow from as far out as the channel of the river. Always heard it said before that if you was to lose some part of your body that something would be given in return. Never used to believe it. But I do now. I believe it with all my heart. I'd probably still be a deckhand today if the power of that lost leg hadn't gone to my eyes."

Jeb looked at the small man that guided the great boat. He thought again of the stubtail and white eye of the hound. He was more sure now than ever before that something would be given in exchange for them. And he knew now that Grandma Quildy and the print of the Book had been right. On top of a mountain, a man would have his legs to judge the ground underneath his steps. On the river, his legs would be useless, except to stand on. The keenness of his eye would be his strength.

At first, Jeb thought the trip down river would be the longest trip he would ever take, but now it seemed short. Already Captain Peg was guiding the boat toward a wooden wharf that stuck out from the bank. The sun had broken over the water and Jeb had not even noticed it. Now it stood over his head. The race would be run in the early afternoon and Jeb knew, as he looked toward the sky, that time was not very far off. The boat slid beside the wharf and two men stretched the board from the deck of the boat. Jeb looked at the red hound and started for the door.

"Be looking for you at dusk, Jeb," Captain Peg said, grinning. "You know...," he ran his hand over his chin, "I've been guiding this boat up and down this river for thirty years now and I reckon tonight will be the first time I've ever had a real champion on board."

Jeb left the pilothouse and went down the ladder.

Chapter Twelve
THE GIFT
■

The way to the championship race was well marked. Signs with arrows led Jeb and Jeptha across the small town of Oakport and more than two miles up a dirt road. Jeb walked behind Jeptha, leading the red hound again with a rope. The hound had gotten used to the lead now and he walked beside Jeb, leaving slack in the rope.

They reached the Leafy Oak Farm just as the sun started down the other side of the white clouds. There was an oak arch gate that opened to the farm and banners and flags hung from the gate post. Jeb walked inside the gate and followed Jeptha toward a small woods where he could see people standing. Getting closer, he saw that a number of tents had been pitched, according to Jeptha, for people who had spent the night to rest their hounds for the race. There was a hound tied to almost every tree and Jeb looked with his eyes wide. But according to Jeptha, all the hounds that he saw would not be entered in the great race. Some would be sold to men that had come to buy

The Gift

as well as watch the race. Jeb was glad that all of the hounds would not enter the race. There were more hounds than Jeb had ever hoped to see at one time.

The red hound crowded close to Jeb as Jeb walked through the crowd of people. Under a tall black oak, a man sat at a table, and over the table hanging from one of the black oak limbs was a sign that read: PAY ENTRY FEE HERE. Jeb turned toward the table.

Jeb walked up to the table as a man was leading a hound away. On the hound's side was painted the number six. The hound sniffed at the paint as he walked and pulled at the hair with his teeth. Jeb led Mooneye up to the table and stood in front of the man.

"My name is Jeb Lockwood," he said. "I have brought my hound Mooneye from the Big Sandy country to enter in your race."

The man scribbled something on a piece of paper and looked at Jeb and then at the red hound. He grinned and then broke into a big smile.

"Jeb Lockwood," the man said, looking through a stack of papers on the table. He pulled out a sheet. "Here it is. From the Big Sandy for sure. Got your letter all right. Glad you could bring your hound, Jeb. My name is Zack Hewlett." He stretched his hand over the table and shook hands with Jeb.

Jeb then laid ten dollars on top of the table. He looked at the ten dollars. He thought of the coonskin, the muskrat hides, mayapple and ginseng and sweet anise root herbs. All of them had been a lot of work. And Grandma Quildy was right…it was a lot of money.

"Good-looking hound, Jeb," Mr. Hewlett said. "You came a long way with him." And then he stooped and patted Mooneye on the head. Mooneye trembled and Mr. Hewlett painted the number seven on his side. The red hound flinched with each touch of the brush and looked toward Jeb and whined. Then he pulled at the paint with his teeth.

"He has got to have a number for the race," Mr. Hewlett said. "The paint will come off. Wish you luck. Would say I hoped you'd win but I'm afraid Blue Night, over there, might get mad knowing I was wishing against him." Mr. Hewlett pointed toward the large bluetick hound that stood under a beech tree close to the table. The large bluetick sat eyeing the red hound. "Man wouldn't be much of a hunter, I reckon, if he couldn't have faith in his own hound to win, could he? Blue Night will be trying today for his second state championship."

The Gift

The bluetick was the largest hound Jeb had ever seen. Long, blue spotted ears dropped almost to the ground and he was broader across the chest than the bulldog. His voice will surely shake the woods, Jeb thought, staring at the hound.

"It is a while before the race, Jeb," Mr. Hewlett said. "If your hound is tired you might want to rest him. If he is rested, you might want to walk some stiffness out of him. Or maybe you just want to look around. There is a lot to see."

Jeb walked over to another oak tree and stood looking at all the hounds and people. Jeptha was walking among the trees, stopping here and there to judge a hound.

Finally all of the people started walking across a stubble field toward a large black oak that stood alone at the edge of the field. Jeb walked with them and on the way he overheard them say this would be the tree where the hounds would finish the race. Jeb stopped with the crowd of people about twenty feet from the tree. He looked across the large field. On the other side of the field was a deep woods. Beyond the woods the coon scent would be started. The scent would be dragged through underbrush, over logs, across a stream that centered the woods, and rubbed on the bark of several of the trees to fool the hounds. The track

The Gift

would cover more than two miles of ground, working through the woods to the cleared field. The hounds that were entered in the race would be taken by wagon beyond the woods before the scent would be made across the field and a live coon tied in the black oak tree. In the time it would take the hounds to work through the woods, the owners of the hounds could get back to the tree to watch the hounds break out of the woods and cross the field.

Four men stood beside the tree. Jeb listened as Mr. Hewlett called out their names to the crowd that stood behind a rope fence. One of the men was the field marshal, and the other three were field judges. These men would call out the name and number of the winner and prevent the hounds from fighting when they reached the tree. The track was now being laid at the other side of the woods. As soon as the hounds that were entered in the race had gone, the scent would be dragged across the field.

Mr. Hewlett talked to the crowd about the great race and then one by one he called out the number of each hound. And one by one hounds were taken to the wagon by their owners. Jeb heard the number seven and cold chills swept his body as he lifted his red hound into the wagon and took a seat beside him. Jeptha stood by the wagon and smiled at Jeb. He reached out his large hand and patted the pup's head. Several of the men looked at Mooneye and grinned.

"A hound is as good as his master, Jeb," Jeptha said. "Show him the track and let him know that it is coon."

"Should he tell the hound to wag his tail?" a man in the wagon said. Several of the men in the wagon joined in and laughed.

The smile left Jeptha's face and he looked at the man who was holding a black-and-tan hound beside him. Jeptha stared hard at him, but then his face broke into a grin.

"You ought to be glad the hound is without a tail," he said. "This way your hound won't get swished in the face when the red hound passes him on the trail."

All of the men in the wagon laughed.

"I'll be waiting for the hound at the tree," Jeptha said.

Mr. Hewlett was the last to climb into the wagon. He pointed toward the wagon bed with his finger and the great bluetick lifted as if it had wings and landed on the oak board wagon bed. Mr. Hewlett took a seat beside Jeb and the wagon bounced up the road.

The Gift

Mooneye lay at Jeb's feet and Jeb watched the red hound breathe. Once, he had thought, this would be a time when he would be the happiest boy in the whole world. But he knew now that he had been wrong. He was not happy; he was scared. Around him sat fifteen hunters with their hounds. There was not a hound in the wagon that did not seem twice the size of Mooneye. Each hound had two good eyes and a long tail. And Jeb knew that each hound was seasoned to the trail. Over and over, Jeb thought about what Mr. Tate had once said: "It is not just an ordinary race. It is the best of the best hounds."

Long ears marked every hound in the wagon. The crowd of people had looked at each of them and had spoken words that would have caused Jeb's chest to swell had they said such words about Mooneye. But to Mooneye, they had just pointed at the white eye and stubtail. Once Jeb overheard a man say that a boy had brought a mooneyed hound all the way from the Big Sandy country to try and beat coon dogs. Each hound sat on his haunches as if he were waiting for his master to give the word to go. Mooneye laid with his eyes closed, now and then opening them to look at Jeb and to wag his stubtail. The red hound had traveled without rest. Maybe, Jeb thought, it had

The Mooneyed Hound

been wrong to bring him here to run against hounds that had been trained to run in the daytime; hounds that would break over the field and run for their master instead of for the scent of the trail. Mooneye knew only to run a coon when there was darkness in the woods.

Across Jeb's shoulder hung the hunter's horn. It had been the only horn at the race. A hunter did not call his hound in during the daytime, Jeb had heard men say. And to make it worse, now and then one of the men in the wagon said something about the mooneyed hound. Jeb sat with his eyes down and tried to pay no attention.

"Reckon he could call the hound back with that horn," the man with the black-and-tan hound said, eyeing the red hound. "That is, if the coon was to take a notion to come out of the tree and chase him."

"You mean if he ain't trampled by the hounds before he reaches the tree?" another man said.

"Leave the boy alone," Mr. Hewlett said, looking at Jeb with a smile on his face. "You all just might have to eat your words. I say a hunter with enough faith to come all the way from the Sandy country would bring a true hound with him."

Tears welled in Jeb's eyes. Mr. Hewlett, he

The Gift

thought, was a good hunter. If the bluetick came first to the tree, it would not be hard to pray for him and his hound like he had promised Grandma Quildy he would do. To pray for the man that owned the black-and-tan would take a lot of faith.

The wagon stopped at the far end of the woods. The hounds jumped off the back of the wagon, sniffed the ground, and barked at their masters. Jeb scooted off the wagon and lifted his red hound to the ground. Mooneye wagged his stubtail and hunkered close to Jeb.

Jeb followed the men and hounds to where the scent had been started. The great bluetick was the first to nose the scent. He lifted his head into the air and bawled. And then, one by one, the hounds struck the scent and opened with their voices. Jeb pointed his finger to the ground and Mooneye sniffed and then turned back to Jeb. The hounds turned into the woods and the men climbed back to their seats on the wagon, anxious to get started, so that they would be back in time to see the hounds break across the open field. Mooneye stood, eyeing Jeb as he climbed into the wagon. He looked with sad eyes and would not offer to follow the trail. The men in the wagon laughed as the wagon started off and the red hound started to follow.

"Get him, Mooneye," Jeb yelled, motioning with his hands toward the woods. The wagon moved away.

The red hound stood at the edge of the woods and watched the wagon out of sight. Tears came to Jeb's eyes and he wanted to jump from the end of the wagon and run to the red hound. But Mr. Hewlett's words kept ringing in his ears: "A man that would have faith enough to come all the way from the Big Sandy country would bring a true hound with him." To go get the hound would show that he did not have faith.

Maybe, Jeb thought, as the wagon neared the crowd, Grandma Quildy had been wrong. Maybe the hound had not been given anything in exchange for the blind eye. Maybe the great Samson had not gotten his sight back and had been left to wander blind among the tall trees. Jeb had never seen the land that had been given to Job, and what you couldn't see was hard to believe.

Jeb stared toward the woods. Far away he could hear the bawling of the hounds. He thought of Jeptha who was standing, waiting for the red hound to break across the field. He will not come, Jeb thought. He will not come at all. Maybe Mooneye thought he had been left alone, and that

The Gift

Jeb did not want him anymore. And maybe he would wander over the strange country out of hearing distance of his master's horn.

The wagon stopped beside the crowd and the men jumped out and stood beside the rope, listening to their hounds deep in the woods. Each man cocked his head and called out his hound's name according to the hound's bark. Jeb walked and stood beside Jeptha. Jeptha looked down at him.

"Don't hear the red hound, yet," he said. "He'll open though. He might be waiting until he gets ahead of the other hounds."

"Maybe he won't come at all," Jeb said, tears welling in his eyes.

"Have faith in your hound, Jeb," Jeptha said. "Listen for your hound."

Jeb looked out over the field and listened.

"Blue Night is close to breaking," Jeb heard Mr. Hewlett say.

The bawl of the hounds was close now. They had worked over half of the deep woods and were heading toward the open field. The trees still hid them from sight but before long they would break out into the open. Jeb had never heard so many hounds before at one time. The hound leading the pack, according to the crowd, was Blue Night.

The Mooneyed Hound

Jeb thought again of the small red hound that he had left at the edge of the woods. Mooneye had stood watching the wagon go out of sight. And Jeb had sat on the wagon watching the road and hoping the hound would take to the coon's trail. But he had not come. Jeb looked toward Jeptha. Jeptha kept his eyes fixed on the woods and his ears, Jeb knew, were full of the music of the hounds. Maybe this was a chance to go and get his red hound, Jeb thought. He could slip away from the crowd and go back to the far end of the woods.

Just then, from the edge of the woods, drifted the deep bugle voice of a hound. It was like the bawl of no other. The crowd looked at one another. The bugle voice came again, far ahead of the lead hound in the pack. Over the open field it drifted, past the black oak tree. A smile came to Jeptha's face and he clapped his big hands together.

"Glory be!" Jeptha yelled. "It's the mooneyed hound."

"It's Mooneye, Uncle Jeptha!" Jeb said, returning to the rope.

The bugle voice came again and again. A whisper went over the crowd: "They say it's the mooneyed hound. Couldn't be."

"He's going to break!" someone yelled.

And out of the woods came the red hound. He lifted his head into the air, bawled with his great bugle voice, and stuck his nose back to the ground and ran with the heart of a true hound. His long ears flapped up and down and he bawled with all his might. The bluetick broke and came across the field with lightning speed. Jeb watched with tears in his eyes. Several more of the hounds broke into the open.

Try as they could, the hounds could not match the speed of the small red hound. Across the field he came, lifting his head into the air only long enough to send his bugle voice ahead and let Jeb know he was coming.

He crossed the field ahead of the other hounds and circled the black oak tree. Taking a run, he leaped and pinned his claws into the bark and bawled. The judges jerked the red hound away and motioned approval. The bluetick came in and then the other hounds. They circled and barked at the tree but Jeb did not hear them. He was on his knees, his hands around the neck of the wonderful red hound. Mooneye breathed hard, wagged his stubtail back and forth, and stuck his nose into Jeb's hands.

"What will you do with all of your money, Jeb?" Mr. Hewlett said, a grin on his face.

The Gift

"Reckon I will keep it to raise mooneyed hounds with," Jeb said, hugging the red hound's neck again.

On the bed of the wagon, above the crowd, Jeb stood beside Mr. Hewlett and held Mooneye. The crowd gathered around the wagon and everyone stared at the white-eyed hound. Mr. Hewlett handed Jeb a blue ribbon and the boy's heart pounded with pride and happiness.

"Hunters," Mr. Hewlett said, "I think we have all seen something here today. Not just another winner of the state championship. There have been thirty before this one. But this is the first time in the history of the state that a mooneyed, bobtailed hound has won it. Most of us, I am afraid to say, would have marked this mooneyed hound and destroyed it when it was a pup. I, for one, have learned a lesson. The eye cannot see the heart of a hound. Right now I'd give every dog I own for a mooneyed hound such as this one. It is the first time I have ever see a hound run as if the Lord Almighty was pointing the trail for it. Greatest nose I have ever seen!"

The nose, Jeb thought. All the time it had been the nose. And Jeb knew that it was the greatest gift that could be given to a hound. The Lord had not forgotten the little white-eyed hound. For a

The Mooneyed Hound

minute Jeb felt ashamed. A short time back he wondered if Grandma Quildy had been wrong. He had doubted that Samson had got his sight and Job had got his land. But he would never doubt again. Jeb had searched for faith and he had found it. Right now he could hardly wait to get back to the cabin and tell Grandma Quildy. He could remember her standing in the yard and saying: "God bless you, Jeb, and God bless your mooneyed hound." And they had been blessed. Just like Grandma Quildy had asked them to be.

Jeb did not tie Mooneye to lead him back to the river. The red hound walked beside him, watching Jeb's every step as if he were afraid Jeb might leave him again. Jeptha stopped now and then along the way to shake his head at the hound.

"Wait until Lucy sees the ribbon," he said, laughing. Jeb looked at the ribbon Jeptha had tied around Mooneye's neck.

The boat rested beside the wharf. The plank had been stretched from the boat when the men on the boat saw Jeb, Jeptha, and the hound coming down the bank. The men stood on the deck, squinting their eyes toward the wharf. Captain Peg stuck his head out the small window and waved his hand. Jeptha stepped on the plank.

"Make room for the champion," he said.

The Gift

The red hound walked slowly across the plank, turning now and then to make sure Jeb was behind him.

"Up here, Jeb," Captain Peg yelled when Jeb reached the deck.

Jeb looked at Jeptha and grinned.

"The boys are mighty proud, Jeb," Jeptha said.

The men stood in a row and Jeb and the red hound walked between them. He climbed the ladder with Mooneye and walked into the small pilothouse. Captain Peg looked at the blue ribbon and patted Mooneye on the head. And then he looked out the window at his men.

"Pull in the plank, men," Captain Peg yelled. "Untie the ropes." He reached over his head, pulled a cord, and the low whistle of the boat horn drifted over the river.

Captain Peg looked at Jeb and smiled.

"Let's take the champion home," he said.

The great paddle wheel churned the water, and the boat nosed up current toward the Big Sandy River.

Billy C. Clark
Copyright © 1985, The Couier-Journal. Reprinted with permission.

About the Author
BILLY C. CLARK
■

A discussion of Billy Clark (1928-   ) may aptly begin with **A Long Row to Hoe** (1960), a narrative of reminiscences and perhaps Clark's best and most warmly received volume. His seventh published book and the story of his life through high school, it makes clear that the wellspring of his career was his background growing up in a semiliterate, impoverished home on the Big Sandy River near Catlettsburg. The volume tells of a ragged family living at the junction of the Big Sandy and Ohio: an intelligent father, a shoemaker and a fiddle player, whose literacy was limited to signing his name and who told his son about poor people "having a hard row to hoe"; the mother, a laundress who played the piano and was so generous of heart, according to her husband, "She'd give away a chair with someone sitting in it"; and eight children. One of Clark's greatest regrets has always been that his parents were unable to read his books.[1]

"In nineteen years of growing up in the

valley, hunger was my most vivid memory and an education my greatest desire," Clark declares as he tells of how as a boy he trapped for muskrats, set trotlines, salvaged flotsam, and scrounged for whatever small sums of money he could get. It is not psychological scars, however, that Clark writes about but the learning and the lore that came from the rivers, the community, and the people who were a part of his growing up. In fact the *Time* review of **A Long Row to Hoe** (July 25, 1960) concluded that Clark, "far from trying to forget his boyhood miseries...has dignified them through grit and awareness of the natural beauty around him." And the *San Francisco Chronicle* reviewer (Oct. 2, 1960) observed that Clark's reader "comes to the end of his book envious of his opportunity to have had such a wonderful childhood."

After graduating from high school—the point at which **A Long Row to Hoe** ends—Clark spent four years in military service during the Korean War and then entered the University of Kentucky in 1953. He tried to pay his way with the help of the GI Bill, carry on his studies, and do the writing that had been a compulsion even during high school days. Clark says that when he was enrolled in a writing class, "Hollis

About the Author

[Summers] recommended that I drop his class" on the grounds that, "You are the first natural-born writer I've ever met, and your writing is changing in class." But Clark insisted on completing the course, and as his works make evident, he managed to preserve his own way of looking at things and the distinctive characteristics of style and manner that in another writer might be called defects.

During his years as a college student Clark managed to publish *A Heap of Hills* (1956), a collection of stories, and to get ready for a burst of publication—five volumes during the next five years. One was **Song of the River** (1957), a novel he had written when he was a freshman in high school. It is the story of an aging man who lives in a shantyboat on the Big Sandy and whose aim in life is to catch a legendary great catfish known as Scrapiron Jack. The main thread of the story is reminiscent of Hemingway's *The Old Man and the Sea*, but what makes the novel distinctly Clark's own is his detailed portrayal of the life on the river.

In **The Trail of the Hunter's Horn** (1957) a boy, Jeb, has worked long and hard to earn a pup of his uncle's wonderful hound, Lucy, and is bitterly disappointed when the pup turns out to be stub-tailed and blind in one eye. As the novel progresses, however, and in its sequel, ***Mooneyed Hound*** (1959), love between the boy and the dog replaces all other considerations, the animal shows prowess as a coon dog, and Jeb enters him in the annual trials for the best coon dog in Kentucky. Reviewers noted two qualities in these novels that make them something more than just juvenile stories about a boy and a pet. One is the author's sensitivity in developing the relationship between the boy and his dog; the other is his responsiveness to the rugged beauty of the land. "This book," says the *Saturday Review* of the first volume (Oct. 19, 1957), "has a quality of universality which makes it one of those stories which haunts the reader, no matter what his age. It is evident that Mr. Clark loves the hills and rivers and people about which he writes."

Riverboy was published in 1958 and was followed by ***A Long Row to Hoe*** and then by three more volumes that are characteristic of Clark at his best: ***Goodbye, Kate*** (1964), a story of a vagrant mule that becomes a community nuisance; *The Champion of Sourwood* (1966), which tells of an agreement whereby thirteen-year-old Aram Tate agrees to teach a wily woodsman, moonshiner, and cockfighter to read

About the Author

and write if the latter will get Aram a hound dog and teach him about "the varmints and the mountains"; and *Sourwood Tales* (1968), a collection of eighteen stories that picture life in the Big Sandy region during the Great Depression. In all these works Clark's sometimes extravagant yarns hold his stories together, but nothing perhaps equals the author's portrayal of the local life and lore and his responsiveness to the surrounding natural beauty. The sounds of rustic music, the roughhewn and unsophisticated mountain and river characters, and the humor and pathos in human and life situations—these make Clark the chronicler of the Big Sandy region.

William S. Ward

---

*Titles in bold type are in print and available from the Jesse Stuart Foundation.

[1] Quoted from William S. Ward, *A Literary History of Kentucky* (Knoxville: The University of Tennessee Press, 1988), 353-355.

THE JESSE STUART FOUNDATION
■

Incorporated in 1979 for public, charitable, and educational purposes, the Jesse Stuart Foundation is devoted to preserving both Jesse Stuart's literary legacy and W-Hollow, the eastern Kentucky valley which became a part of America's literary landscape as a result of Stuart's writings. The Foundation, which controls rights to Stuart's published and unpublished literary works, is currently reprinting many of his best out-of-print books, along with other books which focus on Kentucky and Southern Appalachia.

Our primary purpose is to publish books which supplement the educational system, at all levels. We have now produced more than thirty editions and have hundreds of other regional books in stock, because we want to make these materials accessible to students, teachers, librarians, and general readers. We also promote Stuart's legacy through video tapes, dramas, and presentations for school and civic groups.

Stuart taught and lectured extensively. His

teaching experience ranged from the one-room schoolhouses of his youth in eastern Kentucky to the American University in Cairo, Egypt, and embraced years of service as school superintendent, high-school teacher, and high-school principal. "First, last, always," said Jesse Stuart, "I am a teacher...Good teaching is forever and the teacher is immortal."

In keeping with Stuart's devotion to teaching, the Jesse Stuart Foundation is working hard to publish materials that will be appropriate for school use. For example, the Foundation has reprinted eight of Stuart's junior books (for grades 3-7), and a Teacher's Guide to assist with their classroom use. The Foundation has also published many books that would be appropriate for grades 6-12, including Stuart's *Hie to the Hunters*, Thomas D. Clark's *Simon Kenton, Kentucky Scout*, and Billy C. Clark's *A Long Row To Hoe*. Other recent JSF publications range from college history texts to books for adult literacy students.

James M. Gifford
Executive Director